Band Geeks

by

Lara Hope Hayes

First paperback edition October 2022

ISBN 979-8-218-09129-3 (paperback)
ISBN 979-8-218-09129-3 (ebook)

For Chuck

Table of Contents

August
1994

Chapter One

It was that time of year again, and Cecilia Banbury found herself standing in the same store she and her mother shop at every year. She glanced across the store, hoping to spot her best friend Lou while her mother sifted through the clothes on the clearance rack. Cecilia and Lou had been best friends longer than either one of them could remember. She is closer to him than she is to her own brother. Lou is so charming and lovable that everyone in town revered his good nature. Unfortunately, he was nowhere in sight, so she couldn't rely on him to rescue her from her mother's poor taste.

"Sweetie, what do you think?" her mother asked cheerfully.

Cecilia stared up at the floral monstrosity her mother had so diligently chosen. She wrinkled her forehead in disgust and shook her head. Usually, she enjoyed shopping and didn't mind spending time with her mom but doing both of those things simultaneously was never fun. Cecilia knew better than to show her mother what she really wanted. She just had to wait until her mother came up with the least hideous thing and compromise from there. If she had shown her mother the cute paisley shirt with the holes cut out of the sleeves, it would have led to a 10-minute rant about "looking like someone's orphan in rags when she is lucky enough to be able to afford proper attire." Cecilia could almost hear the lecture in her head when her mother presented her with yet another fashion nightmare. She couldn't take it anymore.

"Let's just get some jeans and go," said Cecilia as they slowly strolled toward the blue jeans and away from the reject rack.

They spotted Lou coming towards them with an armful of new clothes to try on. Cecilia silently took a couple of shirts off his pile to help lighten the load. He grinned back at her, knowing she hated that he didn't have to shop with his mom.

"Registration is coming up. Have you two decided which electives you want to take?" Mrs. Banbury asked.

"Band and Spanish," Lou proudly reported. His mom was a teacher, so he knew what classes he would take from now until his last year of high school.

Cecilia wasn't sure if she was ready to answer that question. She had been thinking about it. This year she was going to Brementon Junior High School. She wasn't worried about missing her classmates. Brementon is a rather small town, so everybody sticks together from kindergarten up through high school. The new Junior High was just 7th and 8th graders, and everybody got to pick two electives a semester. The classes she had to choose from were like nothing Cecilia had ever seen before. Home economics seemed promising, and her mother always wanted her to learn how to sew. There was an art class, but Cecilia was never very good at drawing. The one time she drew a stick man, it looked like a TV antenna. There were also different types of computer classes, from typing to computer graphics.

Her mother's voice suddenly interrupted her train of thought. "You know, Arion started in the concert band when he was in the 7th grade."

Cecilia was waiting for her mother to mention her brother's name. He plays football in the fall and plays in the concert band in the spring. She dreaded the day she would have to decide what electives to take because she knew her mother would pressure her to follow the same musical path as her overly talented brother. Last year the high school concert band got superior marks at the Spring Contest against a bunch of other high schools. It was supposed to be some kind of big deal. Cecilia remembered her parents dragging her to all of Arion's football games, concerts, contests, parades, and even performances at local churches.

She thought of the time Arion and a few of the other high school band students came to visit the middle school. Each student had an instrument, and they stood up in front of all the sixth graders and did a demonstration. A student presented each instrument, and they all played together at the end. Of course, Arion brought his trumpet. Some of the students had two instruments. One girl had a regular flute and a tiny one called a piccolo, and she could play both of them. One boy had a curly brass horn called a French horn, and he also had what looked like a big trumpet, but it was a French horn too. The curly one was for concert, and the trumpet-looking one was for marching. That perked Cecilia's interest. The only part of Arion's football games she liked was the halftime show. She could never follow the game itself, but she never missed the color and sound of the marching band.

During the game, Cecilia knew when something important happened when she heard the band play the fight song. Everybody clapped and cheered for the team, and she clapped for the band. Unfortunately, marching band was strictly for high school students. Students are required to participate in beginner and advanced concert band to get into marching band.

They got to the dressing area, and Lou took his things to the boy's side, "You know, Cecilia, band isn't just for geeks. Besides, it would be fun to do it together."

"Here," her mother handed her two pairs of jeans, "Think about it while you try these on."

After she closed the stall door to the little dressing room, Cecilia tossed the jeans onto a chair and stared at herself in the full-length mirror. She saw an average young girl standing there. She wasn't exceptionally tall or exceptionally short, for that matter. She was not beautiful, but she was also not ugly. She did have long toes and knobby knees, but she was not self-conscious about either of those features. Even her hair seemed to be average and plain. She wasn't the smartest person in the world, but she was no dummy either. Cecilia tried to flex her muscles, but nothing happened. She was looking for that potential her parents were always talking about. *What can I do? What do I want to do?* Even after she was done trying on the blue jeans, she stayed in the dressing room and continued to examine herself inside and out. All she could think was *I want to be good at something*. Would it be worth it to endure two years of concert band if it meant that she could march in high school? She took one last look at herself before she stepped out of the dressing room.

"Well?" Mrs. Banbury immediately asked.

Cecilia wasn't sure whether her mother was inquiring about the pants or what class she planned on taking, "Yeah. They fit."

"Good. Now tell me which classes you picked," her mother knew she was trying to avoid the question.

Cecilia looked up and took a slow, deep breath before saying, "Maybe band isn't such a bad idea. It might turn out to be fun. Lou will be there, and Arion seems to like it, but he isn't exactly hard to please. I will try really hard to do well, but if I'm not good at it, you can't be mad at me."

Her mother smiled and said, "Fair enough," and they made their way to the register.

Just as they stepped outside the store, the familiar sound of the church bells filled the air. The large Baptist Church on the square had a tall steeple equipped with an impressive bell tower. Everyone in town could hear church bells toll the hours of the day.

"Oh Gosh," Mrs. Banbury said. "Lou, your mother will be quite upset if I make you late for dinner."

"Me, too," replied Lou. "Spaghetti night."

They jumped in the car and headed for home. The radio in the car didn't work, but Cecilia's mother would sometimes hum a cheerful tune to break the silence. This time she whistled the tune of the Brementon High School fight song, so Cecilia and Lou hummed along.

"Are you really going to take band, or are you just humoring your mom?" Lou asked in a low whisper so Mrs. Banbury wouldn't hear.

"Sure. What else am I gonna do? And anyway, you'll be there," she replied as quietly as possible.

Lou smiled back at her in agreement, and they both silently stared out the car window. She saw the same things out that window every day, but they seemed to get smaller and smaller each day. Everything was overly familiar to the point of monotony. If she didn't recognize everyone she saw, they recognized her because they knew someone she knew or was related to. There wasn't a whole lot to do in Brementon, either. There was a beautiful and expansive lake that was well known for its supply of bass. Some fishermen say that the fish practically jump out of the water the second you decide to throw your line in. Unfortunately, Cecilia's attention span was much too short for a hobby like fishing. The only other thing to do in town was go to the movies, but that gets old quickly. Even though there is almost nothing to do in Brementon, nobody gets too bored because the universal favorite pastime is getting into everybody else's business and creating business for others to get into. It was easy for Cecilia to feel claustrophobic because everything was so connected to her that she could never escape. They pulled up to the house just as she considered running away and joining the circus.

"I can smell dad grilling his delicious bell pepper chicken," Cecilia said as she stepped out of the car and took a big whiff of the smoky air.

Lou quickly collected his purchases, jumped out of the car, and went off toward Cecilia's house.

They didn't go inside right away. Cecilia left the jeans in the car and quickly headed to the backyard. She couldn't remember the last time her father didn't cook dinner on the grill. If it were raining, he would be out there with his umbrella. She liked the smells that came from the hot grill. She could almost taste the warm air.

"Hey," her father hollered across the yard, "How was the big back-to-school shopping trip?"

As they stepped closer to Mr. Banbury, he could see that Cecilia was rolling her eyes. He gave her a quick wink before turning his attention to Mrs. Banbury. He knew how much Cecilia hated shopping with her mother.

"Hey, Mr. Banbury," Lou politely greeted Cecilia's dad before taking a piece of yellow bell pepper off the grill. "Don't worry. I'm not staying. Spaghetti night." He stuffed the pepper in his mouth, waved goodbye, and went through the backyard to his house. He only lived three houses away, and they were allowed to cut through the other yards as long as they didn't trample Mrs. Ruth's garden or tease Dr. Shepard's little dog.

Mrs. Banbury could barely speak fast enough to get her answer out, "We got jeans. Where is Arion? We have news!"

"Mom," Cecilia whined, "Don't make this a big thing."

"I'm not. I'm not. I just want them to know," her mother replied.

Mr. Banbury looked at both of them before asking, "What's all this now?"

Cecilia continued rolling her eyes and said, "It's nothing."

"Where's Arion?" Mrs. Banbury asked again impatiently.

Mr. Banbury kissed his wife on the forehead and replied, "Arion is inside cleaning up for dinner. Football practice ran a little late, so he just got in."

"Talking about me?" Arion appeared behind the screen door and unintentionally scared all three of them.

"I almost dropped that piece of chicken!" Mr. Banbury exclaimed.

"Sorry. I thought I heard my name," Arion replied with a smile.

"You did," Mrs. Banbury blurted, "Cecilia has something to tell us."

Arion glanced at her and said, "It sounds like *you* have something to tell us, Mom."

Mr. Banbury was having a hard time paying attention to the conversation and his bell pepper chicken, "Can we wait until we sit down for dinner to talk about this? It'll be ready in just a few minutes."

"I don't think Mom can wait until then," Cecilia jokingly replied.

"Look, by the time you three set the table, this should be done," Mr. Banbury suggested.

Arion opened the screen door for his mother and sister, but only his mother went in the house, "Cecilia?"

"I want to stay outside with dad," she answered.

As soon as Arion and Mrs. Banbury were gone, Mr. Banbury split a hot grilled bell pepper slice in half and shared it with Cecilia. She knew if she stayed outside, he would give her a bite of whatever he was cooking. Everything she had ever eaten in her whole life had been cooked over hot charcoal, so she was used to it by now. Her friends liked staying over because they knew Mr. Banbury cooked burgers at sleepovers. Some people have tried to mimic his recipe, but nobody in the world can cook up a burger like Mr. Banbury. He will even tell you that the main ingredient is Worcestershire sauce, but the secret to his burgers is not *what* is in them but *when* he puts in the ingredients in. He knew how to make any kind of food taste better than it should.

Cecilia finished chewing the bell pepper and said, "It's good. Is it ready?"

"Yea should be," her father answered as he checked the inside of a juicy piece of chicken, "Hold the platter for me, kiddo."

Cecilia held the platter close to her dad so he didn't have to reach too far. One by one, he placed the steaming hot chicken breasts right under her nose. She thought her mouth couldn't water any more than it already was until he started putting the bell pepper slices on top of the chicken. It was a good thing Cecilia had to use both of her hands to hold the platter up because she wanted to sneak another bite of one of those pepper slices. They walked into the house and saw Arion and Mrs. Banbury seated at the table. Arion was ready to eat, and Mrs. Banbury was ready to discuss Cecilia's potential for musical greatness.

"All right. Sit, sit," Mrs. Banbury quickly directed.

"Okay, Cecilia, dinner has officially begun. Please tell us your big news," Mr. Banbury was curious to see what could have gotten his wife so wound up.

"It's no big deal," Cecilia insisted, "Mom must've had too much coffee today."

"I'll buy that!" her father said with a hearty laugh.

"Come on, Cecilia, tell them," Mrs. Banbury looked as though she would burst from the suspense.

Cecilia looked around at everybody at the table and said, "I've decided to take band this year. So what?"

"So what?" Mr. Banbury started to get as excited as Mrs. Banbury had, "Hon, that's great! That is *so* great! Don't you think this is just great, Arion?"

Arion chuckled, swallowed a mouthful of food, and said, "Wow. That's interesting. I'll tell you that."

"What is *that* supposed to mean?" Cecilia asked loudly, "You think I can't do it?"

"No," Arion continued to chuckle lightly as he spoke, "I just know what you're in for, and I find it interesting that you would want to take this on. What do you want to play?"

"I don't know," Cecilia replied, shoving a bell pepper slice in her mouth so she wouldn't have to answer the question.

"Please pick something cheap," Mr. Banbury jokingly remarked. "Oh, I'm kidding. Pick whatever you like best. You have some time to decide."

"I told you we had news," Mrs. Banbury was beaming with pride.

"This is big news," Arion stopped laughing and looked at Cecilia, "I'll help you."

"Help me to do what? You are a senior this year and captain of the football team. You won't have time to help me," Cecilia replied.

"Hey now," Arion was trying hard to sound like a caring older brother, "I can't be gone all the time. When I am here, I will help, okay."

Cecilia wasn't going to rely on her brother, but she gave him a quick "Okay."

"See, Hon," Mrs. Banbury was smiling so wide that it looked like she could swallow her ears, "This will be good for all of us!"

Cecilia looked across the table at her brother as he shoveled more food into his face. She knew he was talented. Everybody knew it. He was good at everything he ever

tried to do. Cecilia was more determined than ever to succeed because she wanted to see her parents drag Arion to her concerts, performances, and other functions.

"I think Mr. Hamlin is teaching concert band at the new Brementon Junior High," Arion stated after he swallowed his food.

"What? Sylvester Hamlin is a good teacher!" Mrs. Banbury exclaimed.

"Oh, he is," Arion said. "He taught me how to play the trumpet."

Cecilia's curiosity got the better of her, and she had to ask, "What's he like?"

"He's pretty cool, actually," Arion stated reassuringly, "He's a good musician. He prefers brass, like trumpets, but he can pick up any instrument and play it like a pro. He's laid back while the class is still learning how to read music, but once you pick up an instrument, he gets very intense. He is serious about making sure everybody practices at least 30 minutes every day."

"I remember he had a special form for you to record when you practice, and I had to sign it every week," Mrs. Banbury cheerfully recalled.

"You're kidding! That's silly," Cecilia said with a giggle.

"You'll see. It sounds like fun now but wait until you have to make yourself play every day. 30 minutes of practice seems like an eternity when you only know how to play 'Mary had a Little Lamb,'" Arion explained.

"Come on now," Mr. Banbury said to Arion, "Don't discourage the poor girl before she even gets started."

"Like I was trying to say," Arion continued, "Mr. Hamlin is really big on exposing the class to all different kinds of music. While everybody is coming into the band room, he usually plays something on the stereo, and it's different every day. He does that a lot during the first few classes, and he usually plays something when the class is taking a test."

"Test?" Cecilia could not believe her ears, "How can you take a test in band?"

"Are you kidding?" Arion answered with a grin, "It is like any other class. I mean-- you need a grade, right? Before you learn how to play, you have to take tests where you identify notes, various musical symbols and define some terms. After you learn to play, you have to take tests where you play scales and songs from memory."

Cecilia just stared at her brother with a blank face. What he was talking about sounded like learning a different language instead of band class. She didn't want to give up before she tried, but it was impossible to ignore what he said. She was determined to suffer through practice and even tests if it meant that she might one day march during halftime at a football game.

Arion finished one last enormous bite of food before asking, "Are we done? My show is on."

"Sure. Put your plate and silverware in the sink for me," Mrs. Banbury said.

Cecilia didn't wait for her parents to ask whether or not she was still sure about her decision, "I don't care what Arion says. I still want to do this."

She cleared her plate and went right up to her room. She put her pajamas on and sat on the end of her bed. She kept weighing the work of beginner concert band against the benefits of eventually marching. It was clear to her that the goal might be worth the

consequences, but she was going to do it right and make sure she did everything she was supposed to do, including practice.

Chapter Two

The few days leading up to the start of school seemed to fly by, but the night before the first day of classes was the longest night of Cecilia's life. She kept having dreams that she showed up to school on the last day and had to do all the work for the whole year in one day. She would wake up in a sweat and look at the clock, but only minutes had passed. After waking for the third time, she went to the kitchen for a glass of milk and half a peanut butter sandwich.

It was two o'clock in the morning, so she quietly slipped down the stairs. As she tiptoed around the corner, she noticed that the kitchen light was on. She squinted in the light and continued silently through the hallway.

"What are you doing up?" Arion startled her, but she didn't make a sound.

"Can't sleep," she kept her answer short and quiet.

"Yea. I'm anxious about tomorrow, too. It's my last year, you know," Arion spoke just above a whisper, "I am excited, but it is also depressing. I may not see some of my friends after this year."

"Hey, I wish I was done with school and about to graduate," Cecilia tried to cheer her brother up.

"Just make sure you graduate," Arion instructed in as much of a big brother tone as he could manage under a whisper.

The room was silent while Cecilia got the bread and a knife. She made a whole peanut butter sandwich and gave Arion half. They both finished their snack before speaking again.

"Is band hard?" Cecilia asked.

"Not really," Arion took a swallow of milk, "If I can do it, then I'm sure you can pull it off."

"I want to march," she mumbled softly.

"You can't do that until 9th grade," he explained.

"I know, but I have to start somewhere." Cecilia couldn't extinguish her curiosity, "I wonder what it's like."

"I can't help you there. I'm in the locker room when the band is on the field," Arion answered.

Cecilia was starting to feel sleepy. She yawned and stretched as she stood up from the kitchen table. Arion followed her out of the kitchen, turning the light out as he left the room. They quietly crept up the stairs and went to their rooms. Cecilia went right to sleep after her midnight snack and the chat with her brother. By the time she woke up the next morning, she felt rested, but she was still a bit nervous and excited about her first day back to school.

Mrs. Banbury knocked on Cecilia's bedroom door, "You up, Hon? Breakfast is ready."

Cecilia had to answer, or her mother would come in and pull the sheets off of her, "I'll be right down."

Cecilia put on one of the pairs of blue jeans she and her mother bought the week before and randomly selected a t-shirt out of her dresser. She wasn't too concerned about her clothes because she was focused on seeing her old friends and maybe meeting new ones. She ran out of her room and almost crashed into Arion on her way to the stairs.

"Whoa! Hungry, are we?" Arion was rather chipper despite the early hour.

Cecilia didn't respond. She continued to barrel down the stairs and came to a screeching halt in the middle of the kitchen.

"Where's your brother?" Mrs. Banbury was ready to get her day started.

"Right behind me," Cecilia said just as Arion entered the room.

"All right, big brother, you get to take your little sister to school," Mrs. Banbury said with a smile.

"What? You mean just for today, right?" Arion did not sound happy with his mother's instructions.

"Nope. Your father and I gave you the old station wagon with the understanding that you would help out. Taking your sister to school is a big help," Mrs. Banbury had been waiting for this moment ever since they gave Arion the car earlier that summer.

"But what if this new errand makes me late for class?" Arion asked, "And what about football practice after school?"

Mrs. Banbury was prepared for Arion's attempt to shirk his new chore, "Look, kiddo, you're a senior. I think you can handle waking up 15 minutes earlier to take care of your responsibilities and make it to class on time. Cecilia can ride home with Lou and his mother or catch the bus."

Arion rolled his eyes and then looked at his sister. Cecilia finished her pancakes and stood up with a small piece of bacon sticking out of her mouth.

"Get your stuff. Let's go," Arion said in an exasperated tone.

Arion and Cecilia did not speak during the short ride. Arion was upset at how his mother had tricked him into taking his sister to school, and he was not in a talkative mood.

As they pulled up in front of Brementon Junior High, Arion finally spoke, "Here we are. Have a nice day. See you at dinner."

"You know this wasn't my idea," Cecilia responded.

"I know. I just have to get used to the new routine, that's all," Arion was trying to lighten his tone so Cecilia didn't have a bad start to her day.

"Thanks for the ride," Cecilia said politely as she closed the car door.

She turned and faced the front of the school. It had just been built, and there wasn't time for an open house or anything, so this was her first glimpse at Brementon Junior High School. It was humongous. Even from the sidewalk, she had to crane her neck all the way back to see the top of the building. As her eyes traveled down, she saw the school's name etched in large letters across the front, and further down were impressive white columns acting as both support and decoration. Before walking toward the stairs, she had to take a long, deep breath to prepare for the adventure ahead.

The second she walked through the large front doors, she recognized the tiny figure standing in front of the main office. Cecilia had known Lorelei Besset since elementary school. She had always been very short and very skinny—they thought something was wrong with her when she was younger because she just didn't seem to grow. Nobody would be able to notice her at all if her hair weren't such a rich shade of brunette. Lorelei was known for being very energetic. She always spoke too loud, even when she was trying to whisper. Some may stoop to call her a spaz, but Cecilia appreciated Lorelei's free spirit.

"Hey there, Cecilia! How was your summer?" Lorelei's question echoed in the big entryway.

"Hi, Lorelei. Summer vacation seemed shorter than usual this year," Cecilia said. "Who do you have for homeroom?"

"Not sure. That's why I'm standing here. I lost that letter they sent with all the class information on it. Someone went in the office to find out where I'm supposed to go," Lorelei bellowed in response.

Before Lorelei could finish her sentence, a woman stepped out of the office with a sticky note stuck to the end of her index finger, "Here you go, Miss Besset. Report to Mrs. Tallbay for homeroom, and she will give you your class schedule."

"That's where I'm going," Cecilia smiled at the woman, "We can walk together." The woman went back into the office without another word. "She's a caring staff member. What if we get lost or something?"

Lorelei interrupted Cecilia's complaint by simply pointing to a nearby sign. Cecilia looked around and noticed little directional signs all over the hallway walls. Some of the teachers were standing outside their doors to help students find their way to homeroom. It would have been a challenge to get lost. Before Lorelei and Cecilia reached Mrs. Tallbay's classroom, they made a quick stop in the ladies' room, which was very well-marked, by the way.

Standing in front of the little mirror over one of the tiny sinks was Trilby Euterpek. She was taller than anybody else that Cecilia knew. Her hair was so blonde it was almost transparent. Cecilia remembered how it seemed that Trilby had always worn makeup. Her older sisters used to dress her up like she was some kind of doll when she was little. She didn't feel like herself without some color on her face. When Cecilia stayed over, Trilby would be glamorous even when she was sleeping. She was carefully applying her eye makeup when she looked over at Cecilia and Lorelei.

"I can't stand these tiny school mirrors. I can't see how adorable my outfit looks with this color eye shadow," Trilby was obviously happy despite her reflective dilemma.

"You know you always look good," Lorelei's voice was thunderous in the little bathroom.

"Hey Trilby, cute shoes," Cecilia knew better than to greet Trilby without complimenting her.

"So, one of my sisters got a job at a department store makeup counter," Trilby started talking as if the three of them had been having a conversation all morning, "And she got all new makeup with her discount and gave me all the stuff she was getting rid of."

"Man, I wish I had older sisters," Lorelei couldn't help but say, "All I have is my crumby little sister. She isn't giving me makeup because all she wears is that crazy glitter lip-gloss."

Trilby gave Lorelei a big smile, "Well, this isn't glitter. It's a shimmer, almost metallic."

Cecilia rolled her eyes, "Where are you headed?"

"I've already been there," Trilby was an overachiever, and showing up for school early was part of her routine, "Mr. Frode for homeroom. He won't give me my schedule until the rest of the class shows up. I must have asked him ten times. I think that's why he suggested I go for a walk and learn where everything is, like the bathroom."

"We've got Tallbay," Lorelei seemed to scream her response at Trilby.

"I know where her room is. I can show you," Trilby was more than happy to strut around and show Cecilia and Lorelei that she did know where everything was.

"Hey, Cecilia, are you in there?" came a boy's voice from outside the bathroom.

She immediately recognized the voice, "Yeah, Lou. Be right out."

Trilby glared wide-eyed in the direction Lou's voice came from. She quickly turned back to the mirror for one last opportunity to perfect her appearance. Practically

all the girls Cecilia's age had a crush on Lou. He was charming but also respectful. He acknowledged all the girls as friends but never designated anyone as his *girl*friend. Despite this, Trilby still tried her best to get his attention.

Lou greeted the three girls as they stepped out of the restroom, "Good morning, everyone."

"Hey, where are you headed?" Cecilia asked.

"Uh, Frode," he responded.

"Me, too!" Trilby exclaimed. "We're going there now."

Cecilia and Lorelei shared a giggle as they all made their way down the hall.

Trilby couldn't help but brag, "Even though I don't have my schedule, I know I got one of the electives I picked because I spoke to Mr. Hamlin when I got here this morning."

Cecilia recognized the name, "You're taking band? I picked band, too!"

"All my sisters are in chorus, but I can't sing like any of them," replied Trilby.

"Looks like the three of us will have at least one class together because I also chose band," Lorelei roared.

"Make that four of us," corrected Lou.

"But there is a maximum number of students for each class. You don't know for sure until you get your schedule," Trilby continued to instruct her friends as they came to Mrs. Tallbay's classroom door.

"Thanks, Trilby. I guess we'll see you guys in band," Cecilia wanted to get into the classroom and claim a seat in the back.

"See you then," Lorelei yelled as Trilby and Lou disappeared into their own homeroom.

"Good morning, girls," Mrs. Tallbay greeted Cecilia and Lorelei warmly, "Just pick a seat. This is only homeroom, so you won't be here very long. After everybody else arrives, I'll pass out schedules."

Only three other people were there, so there was plenty of room for Cecilia and Lorelei to sit next to each other in the back row. Cecilia began digging through her backpack to make sure she had some paper and pencils. She looked over at Lorelei and noticed that she was completely empty-handed. No bag, no paper, not even a single pencil.

"Uh, where is your stuff?" Cecilia couldn't help but ask.

"What stuff? Nothing happens on the first day," Lorelei replied to Cecilia, but the whole room heard her, "Besides, it looks like you have enough to share."

"Here is a pencil and three sheets of paper," Cecilia put the school supplies on Lorelei's desk.

When Cecilia turned toward Lorelei, she looked past her face and out the classroom door. She saw a wave of students suddenly filling the hallway. The buses were beginning to arrive and unload everyone at the school. Lorelei noticed Cecilia looking over her shoulder, so she turned her head and saw all the students too. Some faces were familiar, and some were new, but one thing was certain… school was officially back in session.

As soon as everybody was seated and accounted for, Mrs. Tallbay began passing out class schedules. Cecilia was glad her last name started with a *B* because she was one of the first to get hers. She was relieved to see that she had gotten the electives she wanted, but she was disappointed that she had to sit through all her academic classes before going to band and home economics. Lorelei tapped Cecilia's shoulder, and the two

traded schedules. Cecilia noticed that she had a few of her classes with Lorelei, including band. They traded back when the bell rang.

"All right, that's the bell. Good luck on your first day. I'll see some of you later for english," announced Mrs. Tallbay as the students filed out of the classroom.

When Cecilia heard this, she glanced at her schedule and saw that she would return to Mrs. Tallbay for english, which also happened to be right before band. Cecilia looked up at the classroom numbers to make sure she was still going the right way. She stepped into Mr. Duke's science class, took a seat at the back of the room, and folded her arms over her chest. It was going to be a long day.

It felt like two days had passed before Cecilia returned to Mrs. Tallbay's room for english. It took her a few minutes to get there because she was coming from Miss Bilge's class and the math hall was on the other side of the building. There was only one desk left, so Cecilia was forced to sit closer to the front of the room than she liked. Both Trilby and Lorelei were already seated on the other side. When Cecilia looked over, they both smiled at her, and Lorelei gave a friendly wave.

"Welcome to fourth period English," Mrs. Tallbay said as she wrote her name in the middle of the blackboard, "This will be your longest class period of the day because you will have lunch during this hour—which makes it feel like the shortest period of the day because it is harder to get class work done. This means you must do your homework so that everybody knows what is going on during class...."

Cecilia liked Mrs. Tallbay, and that made it easy for her to pay attention. It also made the class period go by quickly. Before she knew it, lunch was over, and the fifth-period bell was about to ring. She looked around the room and noticed that everyone had already packed up their things, but they were still listening intently to Mrs. Tallbay.

When the bell rang, Cecilia almost exploded out of her desk. Fortunately, nobody noticed because everyone else reacted the same way. She shot out of the room so fast that Lorelei and Trilby had to walk quickly to catch up with her.

"I can't walk like this in these shoes," Trilby whined, "Can we please slow down? The tardy bell won't ring for another four minutes."

"We're almost there," Cecilia responded excitedly.

When they got closer to exploratory hall, they saw all the other seventh graders milling around in the hallway and slowly finding their way to class. The music hall was at the end of exploratory hall, so they stuck close together as they made their way through all of the other students.

Partway through the hall, Cecilia swore she heard someone call her name, "Did you hear that?" She stopped and looked around but didn't see anyone she knew. Before she could walk away, she heard it again.

"I didn't think you were going to stop," said a voice that Cecilia immediately recognized, "Don't tell me you are in a hurry to get to class, you big geek!"

"Hey, it's Caroline!" Lorelei's boisterous voice was well-heard in the crowded hallway.

"How was your summer?" Cecilia asked.

"Great," Caroline replied, giving Cecilia and Lorelei a big hug. She was very affectionate and hugged everybody, including teachers. "You know we

moved to that new subdivision, and I have all kinds of people to hang out with now. The only downside is that the neighborhood pool water eats my red hair and turns it eight shades of green."

"I was going to ask about that, but I didn't want to be rude," Lorelei said.

"Where're ya'll going?" Caroline asked.

"The music hall. You?" Cecilia and Lorelei spoke at the same time.

"Same," Caroline responded, "Hey, are ya'll in chorus too?"

"Nope." Lorelei answered before Cecilia could open her mouth this time, "We're in band."

"We can still walk together," Cecilia was happy to run into another friend of hers, but she was still very anxious to get to the band room.

They followed each other through the crowd and came to a stop in front of the music hall. It wasn't much of a hall. The classrooms Cecilia had been in all morning were bigger than that hallway. There were only two doors diagonal from each other and a water fountain at the end of the hall. It was less marvelous than Cecilia had pictured, and she hoped the band room would be a little more impressive.

"I hate to run, but I want to get in here," Cecilia said to Caroline as she moved closer to the door clearly marked: BAND ROOM.

"Nice to see you again, too," Caroline said sarcastically.

Cecilia spun around, "I'm sorry. I guess I'm overly excited. Why don't I call you after school?"

Caroline wrote her phone number on the back of Cecilia's hand with a ballpoint pen, "Now that we go to the same school, we can hang out more."

Trilby leaned toward Lorelei's ear and quietly asked, "Who is that?"

"Oh," Lorelei exclaimed, "I thought you two knew each other."

"Yeah, introduce them," Cecilia said as she started to walk backward toward the door like a magnet was pulling her.

"We'll be right in," Lorelei said before returning to her social duties.

Cecilia reached to turn the doorknob, but the door seemed to open magically without her touching it. She thought it was destiny showing her that she had made the right choice until she was suddenly struck in the head by the door. The magic faded as Cecilia stood in the unusually small hallway with her forehead in her hands, trying to catch her balance.

"Oh no," said a concerned voice from the doorway, "I'm going to run you kids off before class even starts."

"This is Mr. Hamlin," Trilby announced proudly.

"Yes, I am," he responded while he tried to get a better look at Cecilia's forehead. "Are you all right?"

Cecilia had to stop and assess herself before she answered, "I guess."

Mr. Hamlin propped the band room door open with a doorstop. "The rest of you had better get moving before anyone else gets hurt," he said jokingly.

Chapter Three

Cecilia stopped just inside the band room door to visually explore the space. The huge room seemed to swallow her whole. It was four times as big as any of the other classrooms she had seen, and the ceilings were twice as tall. She heard a symphony playing classical music on the stereo. She thought she recognized the tune, but students were quickly filling the room, and the chatter was too loud to hear the whole song. The back of the room was stocked with racks of music stands and a few large drums. There was a special area with various cubby-holes used for storing instrument cases. Cecilia noticed a door at the front of the room that led to Mr. Hamlin's office. She did not have to strain too hard to see inside because a large window took up most of the office wall, which allowed her to look in on the well-kept office. As she peered at the items on the desk, it dawned on her that the window was probably there to serve the teacher's curiosity rather than her own. She focused her attention back to the center of the room and she noticed that there were no chairs or desks anywhere in sight. She was about to vocalize her observation when Lou snuck up behind her and goosed her on the arm.

"Ow!" Cecilia exclaimed as she turned to retaliate.

"Where are the chairs?" Lou asked before Cecilia had the chance to get even.

"Dunno. Hey, this is the first time I've seen you all day. This must be the only class we have together," Cecilia said to Lou.

"See, we wouldn't be in any classes together if we hadn't chosen band," Lou observed.

The tardy bell rang. Everybody was standing around in small groups talking about summer vacation and the first day back to school. Mr. Hamlin stood in the doorway and looked in at all the potential that had consumed his band room. Completely undiscouraged by the lack of furniture, he slowly walked to the front of the room and raised the stereo volume. Pretty soon, the music overpowered all of the little conversations, and everyone went silent in defeat. Mr. Hamlin kept his hand on the dial and a devious smile on his face.

Looking at the man, he did not seem like a typical teacher. He was aloof but somehow still a commanding presence in the front of the classroom. He was the first male teacher Cecilia had seen all day who had a full head of hair. He wasn't exceptionally attractive, but someone must have thought he was handsome because he was wearing a wedding ring.

Cecilia turned her attention from the teacher to the beautiful music blaring through the room. She kept thinking that Lorelei probably wouldn't be able to talk over the music at that volume if she tried. It made it impossible not to listen. The music got faster and more intense as the tune of the song seemed to twist and change in the air. Cecilia was listening most intently when Mr. Hamlin decided to lower the volume of the stereo and address the class.

"That was the Brementon Symphony playing 'Nocturne of the Wild Winter,'" he began. He spoke clearly and loud enough for everyone to hear without shouting. "You have all probably noticed that there are no chairs. Literally, people, there are no chairs. They may not be here until tomorrow after school." A low grumble of complaint came from one side of the room. "Complaining won't do anybody any good because nothing can be done except to carry on without chairs. Please, everyone, come closer to the center of the room and kneel, squat, sit, or whatever."

Trilby looked horrified, "I am *not* sitting on the floor!"

"Why not," Cecilia was rubbing the sore spot on her arm, "You know it's clean because it's brand new."

Cecilia heard Trilby huff exasperatedly as she figured out how to sit on the floor without looking ridiculous or messing up her outfit. Cecilia plopped down between Lou and Lorelei. She looked around at the sea of faces. There were more students than in a regular class, and she couldn't imagine how long it would take to do the attendance.

One of the things Cecilia hated most about the first day of school was how some teachers chose to introduce the students to the class and each other. Usually, this bizarre ritual consists of each student having to stand up, say their name, and offer some interesting fact about their self. To Cecilia's dismay, Mr. Hamlin had this very thing in mind.

"All right, people, I'm going to call the roll. When I say your name, please stand, correct my pronunciation of your name, tell us if you have taken any other music classes or lessons in the past, and let us know what instrument you are interested in playing." Mr. Hamlin took a quick breath as he looked around the room to see how the students

were reacting to his request, "This is a beginner class, but I am curious about you and what you know."

Cecilia took a second to think about what she was going to say when it was her turn. She didn't know what to say, but she thought it would be better to mention something than nothing at all.

"Banbury, Cecilia," Mr. Hamlin pronounced her name correctly.

As Cecilia stood, she felt hot blood rushing to her face, which made her as red as Trilby's shimmer lipstick, "Hey. I'm Cecilia. I haven't had lessons before, but my brother has played the trumpet since he was in Junior High. I guess I might play the trumpet too, but I don't know yet." When she sat back down, the blood rushed down her body and out of her face.

"Besset, Lorelei," Mr. Hamlin said.

Cecilia looked over at Lorelei with a smile. She knew that Lorelei would surprise the class and the teacher with her boisterous voice and lively demeanor. Lorelei had never been humble, but she had always been fearless. That's why Cecilia liked hanging out with her.

"I'm Lorelei," she began in her usual tone, shocking the entire class. They didn't expect to hear so much sound come from such a tiny little girl. "I haven't ever taken music before, but I'm pretty sure I want to play the saxophone."

After Lorelei sat back down, Cecilia gave her a friendly giggle in response to her performance. Cecilia noticed that Lorelei didn't blush. It seemed as though she wasn't even nervous about standing up in front of forty-some-odd students and speaking. If Cecilia was addressing more than four people her face would turn beet red, and she would fidget or twiddle her fingers. She had tuned out the attendance ritual until she heard a few students giggling. When she turned to see what was so funny, she was sad to see that the class was mocking a rather large boy whose face had turned redder than Cecilia's ever could. She didn't understand what was so humorous about a guy with a little weight problem. Trilby obviously got the joke because she was poking Cecilia in the ribs to make sure she noticed the recent spectacle.

"My name is Leo Ephrem," said the boy softly, "I don't know anything about music, and I don't know what I want to play." He shrugged slightly as he spoke and then sat down as if he were trying to disappear into the floor.

Trilby hopped to her feet when she heard Mr. Hamlin stumbling over her last name, "I'm Trilby Euterpek. My last name is pronounced: yew-tur-peck. All of my sisters are in chorus, but I can't sing. I have always wanted to play the flute." She made sure that she made a slow turn while she spoke so that everyone could see how well-dressed she was and carefully sat back down.

Cecilia rolled her eyes at Trilby, "This isn't a fashion show. It's band."

Trilby shook her head with a smile and said, "Hey, I made a better first impression than you did. Besides, the only time you'd ever wear something like this is if you were dead. Just because you live in a house with a couple of guys doesn't mean you have to dress like one."

"I do not dress like a boy. I am casual." Cecilia wasn't offended in the least. "How long does it take you to get ready in the morning? I am up and out the door in less than fifteen minutes at the most."

"It's worth the effort if it gets everyone's attention," Trilby was used to competing for attention at home, so it was natural for her to do so at school as well.

"Ladies," Mr. Hamlin scolded, "It's obvious you two know each other, so why don't you pay attention to the students who you may not know yet? Do you know the name of the young man standing right there?" Mr. Hamlin pointed to a little dark-haired boy in the center of the room.

The boy waved heartily in the girls' direction and introduced himself before they were embarrassed any further, "Me llamo Sonoro Kinney. My friends call me 'Soni.' I love music, but I have never had a class. I am excited about taking band, but I don't know what instrument to play."

Mr. Hamlin continued with the role now that the room was silent again, "Lirit... uh, help me out with the first name here, please."

The girl sitting in front of Cecilia shot to her feet and answered, "My name is Thamyra Lirit." Cecilia jumped in surprise. She could not believe how loud the girl spoke, much more so than Lorelei. "It sounds just like it's spelled: Tha-my-ra. My mother teaches piano lessons and taught me to play as soon as I was old enough to learn how to read music. My father plays the trombone in the local symphony, and he tutors members of the bass section at Brementon High. I want to play trumpet."

Cecilia looked over at Trilby and Lorelei so they could see her cross her eyes. She was not impressed with Thamyra's musical resume. When she returned to the floor, Cecilia stared at the back of her shirt and tried to imagine what it would be like for the unfortunate soul that would have to sit next to that know-it-all. Constantly being corrected and told what to do, the thought irritated her to pieces.

"Finally, an easy one," Mr. Hamlin said in a relieved tone. "Swain, Lou."

Lou quickly stood up and gave the whole class a big fat smile, "I'm Lou. This is my first band class, but I know I want to play the trumpet."

Cecilia noticed Trilby prop herself up so she could get a good look at Lou before he sat back down. She must have felt Cecilia's gaze because she immediately glared back. Cecilia just shook her head in a disapproving yet playful manner.

"Last but not least," Mr. Hamlin began with confidence and then slowly broke off into silence. "Another toughie," he looked up at the class and then back down at the piece of paper in his hand, "Yin, Aki."

A very tall and very skinny black boy stood up, saying, "That's it. You did pretty well. Nobody gets it right the first time." His voice was unusually deep for a young boy, but Cecilia couldn't imagine anyone making fun of him for it. "I am Aki. Music has always been important to me, but I have never learned to play anything. I've always wanted to play drums."

Mr. Hamlin set the roll down and looked up at the class, "I am Mr. Hamlin. I have been teaching young people concert band for twelve years. I have always worked here in Brementon, but I have moved around from the middle school to the high school and now to this new junior high. I also teach the advanced class, but the beginner class has always been my favorite. I hope you expect a lot out of this class because I have high expectations of you. We have lots of material to cover if you want to be prepared for the spring concert at the end of the year." He paused and brought a box full of books out of his office. "This is your textbook for the first half of the year," He held one of the flimsy practice books up so everybody could see the cover. "The first portion will help me teach you how to read music, recognize symbols, and define terms. The second portion is a practice book that goes with your very first instrument, a recorder."

He went back into his office and brought out a plastic clarinet-type thing that looked like something a troll would play in a fairy tale. Cecilia thought it was a joke. Trilby pinched Cecilia and Lorelei in silent protest of the ridiculous teaching tool.

Mr. Hamlin noticed the class was not too happy with the recorder idea, "Hey, I know it's a goofy looking thing, but if you work hard, you won't have to play it for very long. Besides, it's small. You can hide it in your backpack or something." He put the little toy instrument back in his office and picked up his trumpet. He stood in front of the room and played a quick, jazzy riff. "The fun part comes when I get some high school kids over here. They come and show you their instruments and answer all your questions before you decide which instrument you want to play." He glanced around the room and could tell that most of the students were genuinely excited. "Quickly, before the bell rings, tell me what you think the purpose of music is."

"Entertainment" was the first response.

"Okay, that's a good start," Mr. Hamlin wanted the class to answer him rather than him simply telling them what he knew.

Trilby raised her hand, "Music puts babies to sleep."

"Hey, that's a good one," Mr. Hamlin replied.

"Yeah, but bugle calls wake people up," Thamyra Lirit attempted to challenge Trilby's response.

"All of these are correct answers. Keep them coming," Mr. Hamlin was amazed at how enthusiastic his students were becoming simply by discussing music. Other answers came from all over the room at random:

"Parades."

"Weddings."

"Funerals."

"All right, all those things fit into the ceremony category," Mr. Hamlin coaxed them to think even harder, "What is the purpose of ceremony?"

The room fell silent. Cecilia thought long and hard before thrusting her hand in the air, "It brings people together."

"Excellent! What else can you think of that is important about music?" Mr. Hamlin tried to stretch the discussion for as long as possible because he knew class was almost over. To him, the first day back always seemed to fly by.

Lorelei took a shot at the question, "What about, like, the alphabet song and nursery rhymes and stuff?" She wasn't confident about her answer, so she didn't speak too loudly this time.

"Yes, we use music to teach children the basics of communication," Mr. Hamlin said.

Lou casually put his hand in Mr. Hamlin's view, "Songbirds."

"Oh, animals are nature's musicians. Actually, everything is musical. Tapping, barking, singing, clapping, humming, tweeting, meowing, mooing, clucking, honking, whistling, and whatever else you can think of. The world is made of music. Birds sing on a cloudy day. Crickets chirp on a summer night. People whistle while they work. Mommies lull babies to sleep. A song can make you remember a specific moment in time. It can thunder your very soul or charm you into a trance. Music is one of the world's most available sources of true magic...." The bell cut Mr. Hamlin short. "Grab a book on the way out," Mr. Hamlin announced as he put the box of books by the door before the first student could dash away.

Cecilia took her time making her way to the door. She wasn't as excited about leaving band class as she had been about getting there. Trilby, Lorelei, and Lou waved goodbye before they headed to Spanish. Cecilia perked up a bit when she saw Caroline waiting for her outside the music hall.

"How was it?" Caroline asked.

"Great. I can't wait to get to the good stuff," Cecilia replied cheerfully.

"What do you have next?" Caroline didn't want to walk around alone any more than Cecilia did.

"Home economics," Cecilia said as she double-checked her class schedule.

"Me, too!" Caroline responded almost as loud as Lorelei usually does.

It was a long walk to the home economics lab. Cecilia was grateful to have someone to talk to.

"How is chorus?" Cecilia asked Caroline.

"Okay, I guess. All the girls want to sing the same part, so the teacher has to decide who sings soprano, alto, tenor, blah-blah-blah," Caroline trailed off as she turned her head away from Cecilia.

"What's the matter? You're good. You can sing any part you want," Cecilia tried to sound encouraging, even though she didn't know what she was talking about.

"I just know I am going to get stuck with a bad part. Then I'll get stuck next to the super loud soprano singer with all the solos. I want to sing solos," Caroline whined.

Cecilia couldn't believe that Caroline wanted to sing by herself in front of people. They talked all the way to the classroom door and filed in for the last class of the day.

She stared out the tiny sliver of the window that was visible from her very uncomfortable spot on the floor. She kept thinking about what Mr. Hamlin said about music being everywhere. She wished it was raining so she would have some music to listen to. She was amazed at how he lumped a bunch of different noises into a massive collection of musical possibilities.

"Hey, space cadet. Class is over. Didn't you hear the bell?" Caroline gently nudged Cecilia.

She had been concentrating so hard on finding some music in the room that she completely missed the bell altogether, "Oh man, I've got to meet Lou, or I won't have a ride home." She snatched up her bag and ran to meet Lou in front of the school.

Chapter Four

Since it was the beginning of the school year, Cecilia had plenty of time to study from her band book. At first, she didn't study. She just liked to be seen thumbing through it coolly. But the first note test was at the end of the week, and it was going to be timed. She was excited about taking band class, but she was overwhelmed by all the new terms and weird symbols she had to know.

"This first band test is happening too early. None of my other teachers are scheduling tests so soon. In fact, some of my teachers have hardly assigned any homework at all yet." She was talking to herself, but someone else was listening.

"Hey, squirt. What seems to be the problem?" Arion slid his glass of milk across the kitchen table to where Cecilia was sitting.

"Don't bother me, I'm studying," she quickly answered his question, hoping he would disappear as quietly as he had appeared.

"Yeah, sounds like it. I can help if you want. I mean, it's just the basics," Arion was trying to make his little sister feel better, but he just frustrated her even more.

"You sound like that little twit in my class, Thamyra Lirit. She thinks she knows everything about music. What's worse is she doesn't help anybody or anything. Nope, she just moans and groans about how bored she gets in class talking about all the stuff she already knows." Cecilia's voice got louder and louder as she spoke.

"All right, calm down. What test do you have coming up, treble or bass clef?" Arion made his voice more sincere so Cecilia would know he was serious about helping her.

"Treble, but bass is next week. Not to mention all the symbols and terms I have to know. I'm never going to get to play," Cecilia sounded very discouraged.

"How about I teach you a little mnemonic device I know? It will help you with the note recognition part of the test," he politely offered.

Cecilia thought long and hard. She glared at a page in the book and realized she couldn't do it on her own. She would need help… Arion's help. "I really need help, Arion. What I don't need is you messing with me right now!"

"I won't say a word," he said as he took the pencil out of her hand, "Just watch."

Arion drew five parallel lines across a blank piece of notebook paper. He put circles in the four empty spaces between the lines. He had made a face with the notes on the staff. "See the face, Cecilia? The letters F-A-C-E correspond to the notes in the spaces. See," he pointed to each note in her book.

Cecilia looked at what her brother drew and what was in the book, "Hey, you're right!"

"Don't sound so surprised," Arion felt like a model big brother seated at the kitchen table helping his sister study. "I've got another one for the notes on the lines. It's a little sentence. The first letter of each word corresponds to each note, see: every good boy does fine. E-G-B-D-F," He continued to point expertly at his notes and then at Cecilia's book.

"Wait a minute, *that* is a mnemonic device?" she suddenly realized what the word meant, "I know what that is. Caroline taught me one to memorize the order of the planets. What happens if I forget the sentence?"

"I have a solution to that problem as well," Arion felt very clever answering all of his sister's questions. "See this," He drew a squiggly, curly thing on the staff.

"That symbol is in my book," she was proud of herself for recognizing it right away, "That's the treble clef symbol."

"See, you know this stuff," he said encouragingly. "The curled part of the symbol always wraps around this line," He pointed to the second line up from the bottom. "What note is that?"

Cecilia looked at her brother's finger and thought to herself: *every good boy does fine*, "It's G! The treble clef wraps its curly tail around the G!" She was yelling with excitement.

Arion gave his sister a high five, "I told you that this was the easy stuff. You keep studying that." He strutted proudly out of the kitchen so his sister could concentrate.

Cecilia kept looking back and forth between her book and the notes Arion drew for her. She couldn't believe how confused she was before and how easy it all seemed now. When Arion initially offered her his help, she was tempted to do it alone. The two of them were not famous for getting along, especially after being alone for more than three minutes. She looked up from her books in the direction of the living room. Arion couldn't see her, but she was smiling at him gratefully.

***

The day of the first test came as a relief to Cecilia. Instead of being nervous and anxious, she was relaxed and confident. Everybody except Thamyra Lirit was completely silent. They all had their faces in their books in panicked last-minute preparation.

"I just want to get this stupid thing over with," Thamyra Lirit whined, "As soon as we get done with this baby stuff, we can play."

Trilby was another person in the room that wasn't frantically studying from the book. However, she was filing her nails as intently as anybody else was studying. On the other hand, it seemed as though Lorelei had completely forgotten about the test altogether. She kept opening and closing her book in an attempt to quickly memorize as much as she possibly could. As a matter of fact, the only other person who seemed as remotely confident as Cecilia was Lou.

Suddenly Mr. Hamlin appeared at his office door with a stack of tests in his hand. He placed them on the podium on his way to the big stereo cabinet. He put on beautiful, flowing concert music to get everybody in the mood for the test. It was loud enough for everyone to hear but not so loud that Mr. Hamlin couldn't give instructions.

"Let's get started, gang. I've got a surprise for you when you finish," he was trying to play it cool, but it was obvious that he was excited about something. "Only the first portion of the test will be timed. Consequently, the two portions will be administered separately." Mr. Hamlin noticed a few confused faces, "I'll pass out the note recognition part first. Keep it face down and write your name on the back. When I say 'Go,' you will flip the test and fill in all the blanks as quickly and correctly as possible. When you finish, come forward, and I will record your test time. On your way back to your seat, pick up the second part and take your time defining the terms and symbols as best you can. Any questions before we begin?"

Lorelei spoke up without raising her hand, "What's the surprise?"

Mr. Hamlin chuckled, "If I tell you, then you won't concentrate on your test. I want you all to do well. Just know that you will be rewarded for your efforts." A groan of complaint began to develop, but Mr. Hamlin simply passed out the first part of the test reminding everyone, "Don't flip it over until I say so."

Cecilia remembered that the band room was not equipped with desks. It was full of brand new chairs and old rickety music stands, but no desks. She noticed some of the students turned their stand flat to use as a writing surface. Unfortunately, the stands were metal and bent every way but straight. Mr. Hamlin was coming down the last row, so Cecilia sat straight up in her chair, eager to demonstrate to herself and the class how well she knew her treble clef notes. She got her test and took her time writing her name on the back. Despite her efforts to be neat and careful, the uneven surface of the music stand made it appear as if a small child had written Cecilia's name on her test. She looked at Trilby and Lorelei as a way of saying "Good luck," but both of them were too occupied with their own nervous energy to notice.

"Ready?" Mr. Hamlin asked the class. "Go."

In a matter of seconds, Cecilia's mind was flooded with mixed-up mnemonics. *The good boy has a pretty face. That can't be right*. Her mind was spinning, and she couldn't think of the correct answers. She looked away from the page for a second and took a breath. Pencil in hand, she turned back to her test and immediately scribbled answers as fast as she could think them up. Arion's little trick actually worked. Cecilia thought she was going to be the first one to finish. She glanced at her test one last time to make sure she had filled every answer blank. She got to her feet at the same time as Thamyra Lirit. Unfortunately, Cecilia liked to sit in the back of the room, so she didn't beat her to the podium.

"Congratulations, ladies," Mr. Hamlin wrote the same time on both tests. He saw Thamyra Lirit open her mouth to protest, but he stopped her short, "I watched you both get up at the same time. It's only fair." Cecilia grinned heartily on the way back to her chair while Thamyra Lirit pouted like a spoiled child.

Trilby was next to finish her test, and she took her time getting to the podium to turn it in. Cecilia saw that she was wearing new shoes that were obviously hard to walk in. Even Mr. Hamlin almost giggled, watching her wobble her way to the front of the room. He took her walking time into account when he recorded her time. Cecilia wrote her name on the second part of the test, but she quickly looked up again to see who else was turning in their test. Lou and Aki got up at the same time, but Aki won the race to the podium because he danced his way to the front of the room. Cecilia thought she heard him singing to himself a little bit too. She didn't have to look up when Leo turned in his test because she heard some people laughing. She couldn't feel sorry for him for too long because Trilby was trying to show her that Lorelei was still trying to finish the first part of the test. In fact, Lorelei didn't complete the note recognition test until Cecilia had finished defining all the terms. Trilby shook her head at Lorelei when she stepped over her to turn in her test, and she gave Cecilia a thumbs up.

After everyone had finished both portions of the test and turned them in, Mr. Hamlin turned down the stereo, "We are going to spend the rest of the class period trying to make a final decision about what instrument everyone wants to play. On the first day of class, most of you said that you don't know what you want to play." He tried to play it cool, but he was about to bust, saying, "I thought you could use some help deciding."

Cecilia didn't know what kind of surprise this was, but it wasn't a very good one so far. She had decided to play the trumpet. *What am I supposed to do while everyone is thinking? Listen to Thamyra Lirit whine?* Before she could validate her argument with Trilby or Lorelei, Mr. Hamlin opened the door to the band room. Cecilia heard people in the itty, bitty music hall and watched them enter the room. She suddenly saw what all the fuss was about.

Mr. Hamlin shook hands with a very short, fat man and said, "This is Mr. Alvis. He is the assistant director of the Brementon High Band. As you can see, he brought some of his students with him today to do a little demonstration and answer some questions."

Mr. Alvis didn't say a word, not to the class or his students. He simply pulled a chair to the back of the room and watched silently. Cecilia was amazed. The students knew what they were supposed to do without instructions or anything. It wasn't the whole band, but each instrument was present. They stood in a line across the front of the room and played together. First, they played a warm-up exercise, but Cecilia recognized it as a hymn she had heard before, and then they played the fight song. The whole class was on their feet and clapping.

Once things got quiet again, the students came up one by one to present each instrument individually. The girl with the flute was first, and Cecilia could see Trilby straining to get a better look. She held her flute up and demonstrated how the keys move and where to blow into it. Then she played part of a song, by herself, in front of the whole class. Cecilia couldn't believe her eyes. She kept thinking that she probably wouldn't like having to play for people like that. She didn't like speaking in front of people. How could she play for them?

Next, the girl with the clarinet bounced onto the podium, which made a loud thump when she landed. She tapped her foot the entire time she was on the podium, so it sounded like the loud thump echoed forever. Cecilia listened to the girl, but she was also looking at the boy with the trumpet. He kept wiggling his fingers over the valves and blowing air through it, but no sound came out. Some spit did, however. Cecilia watched in disgust as a tiny wad of moisture dripped onto the floor. She almost forgot about that charming feature—the spit valve.

The tallest boy in the group wore an odd black rope around his neck. When he stood on the podium, he attached his saxophone to a hook at the end. Cecilia thought it was neat that he could wear his horn like a necklace. She knew Lorelei said she wanted to play the sax, but she wasn't paying attention because she was flirting with the guy with all the drums. Cecilia wasn't paying attention to the saxophone player either. She was watching the guy with the trumpet get ready because he was next.

The trumpet player got up on the podium before the saxophone player got off of it. He was cute, but Cecilia could tell by the way he presented himself that he knew just how cute he was. His horn was a brassy yellow, and the bell was dented up pretty badly, but it sounded wonderful. Cecilia didn't care much for what the boy had to say, but she didn't want him to stop playing. He made her think that she could have a chance at being good at something. He only played for a few seconds, but it was enough to captivate Cecilia. She stared at the front of the room with her mouth open, thinking about playing her own trumpet someday.

Her daydream was interrupted by the thick sounds that came from the baritone. He didn't step down when he was finished. He waited for the trombone player, and the two of them played a little something together. They gave each other a high five before the baritone player left the podium. The trombone player showed the class how his horn changed notes with a quick slide rather than pushing valves, like all the other brass horns. Then, instead of playing a song, he made his horn sound like a racecar changing gears. The class was in awe and cheered as he played louder and louder. Cecilia glanced at the back of the room to see Mr. Alvis's reaction, but he just sat quietly with his arms crossed.

The class saw the enormous bell of the tuba before they saw the tiny young man carrying it. He couldn't have been more than four feet tall. Cecilia could barely see him even though he was standing on the podium. Everyone certainly heard the little guy speak—even Lorelei was impressed. The most amazing thing was how effortlessly he hoisted the massive horn up and maneuvered close to the mouthpiece. It was like watching a cartoon in real life. His entire face seemed to sink into the mouthpiece, and his cheeks puffed out to nearly twice their size when he played. The class would have found it funny if it weren't so incredible to watch and listen to. When he finished, he politely bowed, and the class responded with a roaring round of applause.

Lastly, the student with all the drums enlisted the aid of his classmates to get his equipment to the podium. He had three different types of drums and a pair of cymbals. Lorelei was sitting on the edge of her seat and tapping her pencil on the music stand in front of her. Cecilia knew that Lorelei thought the drum guy was hot, but all that wiggling and tapping was about to drive her crazy. She quietly reached over and took the pencil from her. Lorelei must not have realized she was making so much noise because she looked back at Cecilia apologetically.

The drum player had a special thing to wear over his shoulders, holding a drum at his waist. He explained that all the drums he brought sounded very different from one another and that each served its soundful purpose in the ensemble. "The percussion section is like a tiny band in itself because it has so many different parts that work together to produce a wonderful arrangement of sound." Ratta-tat-tat, the snare drum he wore, was loud, and the sound that came from it was very abrupt. The same was true for the quads, but, as the name suggests, there were four drums instead of one. Each drum had a different sound, and none of them sounded like the snare drum. The biggest drum was the bass, which made a loud booming sound that Cecilia could feel shake her heart every time he hit it with the mallet. The last thing he showed the class were the cymbals. He put his hands in the loops at the center of each cymbal and crashed them together. It was the loudest of all the sounds Cecilia had heard that day.

As quickly as it had started, the demonstration was over. Mr. Hamlin made the class clap after everyone had finished. Mr. Alvis was still sitting quietly in the back of the room.

"All right, gang, ever since we got the chairs, I've let you sit where you want, but now I need you to sit according to what instrument you want to play. Flutes in the front row. Clarinets, saxophones, and trumpets are in the middle. The bass section is in the last row. Percussion is in the very back of the room by Mr. Alvis," Mr. Hamlin instructed.

The entire class got to their feet and shuffled around the room to find a new seat. Trilby ran to the front row and got a seat right in the middle. Lorelei couldn't decide whether to sit with the other saxophone hopefuls or to go to the back of the room and flirt with the drummer. Cecilia gave her a fierce snarl of disapproval, and she reluctantly sat in the saxophone section. After everyone was seated again, the high school students went to their respective sections to give everyone a closer look at their instruments and answer any questions.

The trumpet player came over and took a headcount of all the students that wanted to play the trumpet, "Whoa, seven trumpets is a lot for such a small band." He situated himself in front of the students so they could get a good look at his horn and overly attractive face. "My name is Seanán. Just call me Sean. If you have questions, ask one at a time, please." He took the mouthpiece off the horn and handed the trumpet to the first person in the row, "Be careful."

"It's kinda heavy," the boy said as he experimented with each of the three valves.

"You get used to it," Sean replied.

Lou asked the first question, "Hey, Sean, are you missing class right now?"

"Yea, history and computer graphics."

"That is so cool," someone else said.

Sean was more than happy to brag about the fact that he was missing class, "Well, we have to get permission ahead of time from the teacher of each class we will miss."

Lou held the trumpet up to indicate that he had another question, "Why does this part slide? Does it come off?"

"Hey, that's a good question," Sean participates in at least one demonstration a year and always enjoys talking to the students. He reached over and pulled the slide off the horn, "This is the main tuning slide. You adjust it depending on whether you are sharper or flatter than the rest of the section. Sometimes the director will go around and tune the entire band one at a time."

Cecilia didn't like what she was hearing. She wanted to play the trumpet, but not by herself in front of people. Before she said anything out loud, she decided that it wouldn't be that bad if everybody had to do it. Besides, she would have to get over her stage fright before the spring concert. She could practice being cool under pressure during class.

Sean put the slide back on the horn and handed it to the next student, who immediately asked, "What about that thing?" He was, of course, referring to the spit valve.

"That's the spit valve," Sean smiled, "Spit collects in the trumpet while you play, so you just push the spit valve and blow it out."

"That is absolutely disgusting," Cecilia heard someone grumble, and she couldn't help but silently agree.

"Trumpets are not the only horns that have some kind of escape hatch for spit," he explained further, "Baritones, trombones, and tubas all have spit valves. But saxophones have a special hole in the bottom that drips freely. Personally, I'd rather have control over when my valve needs to be emptied and, more importantly, where my spit goes when it falls."

Cecilia had gotten the horn by now, but it was nothing new to her. She had seen Arion's trumpet lying around the house.

She even had to move it out of her way a few times, so she had also handled a trumpet before. This one was a little bit different than her brother's, though. Arion didn't march in the fall, so his horn didn't have much of an opportunity to get dented, rained on, or squished like this one apparently had. Sitting there staring at the trumpet, she finally thought of a question: "Is learning to play the trumpet hard?"

Sean looked up the row at each face in front of him before saying, "I want to say that it's easy, but that's only because I have been playing for a while. I am used to it by now. You know what, though, it doesn't matter if you think it's hard or if you think it's easy. Wanna know why? Because it's so much fun. I know it sounds crazy. Once you start regular practice, you get so distracted by what is going on in class that you can't tell you're working hard."

Mr. Hamlin looked at his watch and addressed the class, "The bell is about to ring. Do me a favor and grab a recorder out of the box on your way out. There
are fingering charts in your practice book if you want to play around this weekend. I want you to have them with you Monday so we can start right after the second test."

Trilby turned completely around in her chair to make eye contact with Cecilia. They were not very excited about carrying such an absurd instrument around. Lorelei didn't seem to mind, but she wasn't paying attention to what Mr. Hamlin was saying. There's a good chance she didn't hear one word. Lou was prepared to endure anything Mr. Hamlin assigned. His mother had molded him into a truly model student.

After the bell rang, it took Cecilia a while to get out the door because she had to wait for everybody to stop and get a recorder. She reluctantly stepped up to the box and looked in. It was half full of pale yellow plastic practice instruments, each conveniently wrapped in its own little clear plastic protective sheath. She stirred them up a bit to see if any were a different color, but there weren't. She took one off the top and stepped out of the way of the people behind her. She took her backpack off to make room for the silly thing so nobody would see her with it. Unfortunately, she had homework in almost every subject, and her backpack was stuffed full already. She continued to rummage around in her bag when two feet stepped up to where she was squatting on the floor.

"We're going to be late for home economics. What are you doing down there?"

Cecilia looked up and saw her friend, "Hey, Caroline. I'm trying to get rid of this ridiculous thing. I guess I'm just going to have to carry it. We only have one class left anyway."

"What is it?" Caroline asked.

"Humiliating, thank you for asking," Lorelei bellowed in protest as she and Trilby came closer.

"It's a recorder. It's only a temporary practice tool," Cecilia explained, feeling like a tool herself as she held it.

Trilby grinned and replied, "I like it. It's kind of like a flute. It has the same whispery sound."

"Well, not everybody wants to play the flute," Cecilia added.

"We have to learn somehow," Lou's voice came out of nowhere.

"Somehow, I knew this wouldn't bother you in the slightest," Cecilia said to Lou. Everyone quickly gathered their things and headed for exploratory hall.

On the way to class, Caroline could tell that Cecilia didn't want to discuss the recorder and quickly decided to change the subject, "How was the test?"

So much had happened since she took the test that she almost forgot about it completely, "Oh, really well. I was one of the first to finish the timed note recognition part. I don't know how I did yet, but I feel good about it. Arion helped me study."

"You're kidding," Caroline said as she helped Cecilia to her feet.

"Nope," she looked at Caroline before finishing her thought, "He taught me some mnemonic devices—my big, mean, nasty older brother."

"Gross!" Caroline exclaimed.

"I know, he is usually very gross," Cecilia tried to continue the conversation, but Caroline stopped her.

"Ew," she pointed, "Look at those guys. The one caught the other one's spit in his mouth."

Cecilia looked in the direction Caroline was pointing. She saw two boys that looked similar, except that one was about two inches taller and a foot wider than the other. The two of them looked like they had been wrestling in the dirt all day rather than sitting in a clean classroom. They both had dark hair, but only one of them had blue eyes. Cecilia recognized them almost immediately, "That's Ben and Moe Ditham. You don't know them?"

Caroline looked at the boys again and wrinkled her forehead, "Is it? I haven't been to school with them since…3rd grade. Wait, Moe is older than Ben. How are they in the same grade?"

Cecilia lowered her voice because they were within earshot of the Ditham brothers, "Moe got held back somewhere along the line, and now he and Ben are always together. Sometimes they try to convince people that they're twins, but everybody knows that they're a couple of troublemakers."

"Whatcha got there, baby Banbury?" Cecilia was familiar with the harsh, raspy voice insulting her. It was Moe Ditham, "Is it a Barbie dream flute?"

"Go away, Moe. I'm already gonna be late for class," Cecilia tried to get rid of him as quickly as possible, but her response only attracted the attention of the other Ditham brother.

Ben stepped closer to Cecilia and his brother, "Boy, you two sure look cute bickering at each other like that. Just like mom and dad used to, aye, bro?"

"Better watch your mouth, man. She's in band. You know those kids are tough," Moe continued mocking Cecilia.

"Yeah," Ben snorted, "If we keep this up, the little band geek might bop us in the head with her gilded horn."

Caroline looked around and noticed that everyone had cleared the hall and made their way to class. The tardy bell could ring any second now. She tugged on Cecilia's shirt and tried to pull her towards the home economics lab. "Come on," she mumbled under her breath.

"No," Cecilia was not going to walk away from the boys' offensive remarks without a bit of retaliation. "Guys like these two heathens have to make fun of people like you and me, Caroline, because they want to make everyone around them just as miserable as they are. I'm going to be good at something while you two are picking each other's noses!"

"Awe," Moe got right in Cecilia's face, "You made the band geek mad, brother. Maybe we can make up for it by whittling her a new little horn in wood shop." He snatched the recorder out of Cecilia's hand and tried to break it over his knee, but the hard plastic wouldn't even crack.

She smirked at Ben and then turned her attention back to Moe, "If you're not going to break it, can I have it back?" Caroline was now pulling her by the arm, so Cecilia seized the recorder from Moe's sweaty grip and ran down the hall. An unknown voice scolded them for running, but it was worth it because they stepped inside the home economics classroom just before the bell rang.

Chapter Five

Cecilia spent most of Friday night and all of Saturday morning finishing her homework. She wanted to use the rest of her free time to practice her recorder. She hated the sight of the stupid thing. She was tempted to hide somewhere while she practiced so nobody would see her, but what could they say? She was doing what she was supposed to, regardless of how weird she looked when she played it.

She sat in her room and quietly studied the first page of the recorder practice section in her book. It had several illustrations that demonstrated how to finger each particular note. The page in front of her contained the fingerings for eight different notes, and she was determined to know them all before school on Monday.

She took the recorder out of its protective sleeve and immediately got an overpowering whiff of the fresh, new plastic. It was brand new, but the yellowish color made it appear aged. She turned it over in her hands to get a better look at the strange device. It had several small holes in front but only one in the back. She turned it back around and tried to hold it the way the diagram suggested.

The cold plastic felt awkward in her hands, but it slowly became warm the longer she held it. She peered down through the small slit in the mouthpiece, but it was too dark to see all the way through with her fingers over all the holes. She looked around to make sure she was alone and blew a light stream of air through the recorder. A whisper of sound tickled Cecilia's hands as it seeped out of the instrument. She had no idea what note she was playing—the important thing was that she was playing *a* note. She suddenly realized how truly silent the room had been before she had played the recorder. She turned her attention back to the book as she carefully followed each diagram and played all eight notes.

"Do I hear someone practicing scales?" Arion shouted from the bottom of the stairs.

The last person Cecilia wanted eavesdropping on her first official practice was her older brother, "I was whistling. Mind your own business."

Despite her efforts to deter him, she heard his footsteps approaching her bedroom door. She tried stuffing the recorder back in its cover, but instead, she almost tore the flimsy thing in half.

Arion flew through the door, making as much noise as possible, "I could have sworn I heard a scale. Are you playing already?" He immediately noticed that Cecilia was hiding something behind her back, "What are you hiding?"

"Oh, nothing," she said, showing him her empty hands.

"No, you're hiding something. Show me, or I'll be forced to perform a tickle tackle." Arion was referring to a tickling game that their parents used to play with them when they were younger. Ever since he started playing football six years ago, Arion had improved the tickle tackle, allowing for much more tackle and a little less tickle.

"I just don't want to show you. Please don't tickle me." Cecilia thumbed through her book as if she were in the middle of doing something very important. "Go away!"

"I know you're practicing up here. It sounded really good," he snuck a quick peek at a page of her book, "I mean, you haven't been in band that long."

Cecilia looked up at her brother shyly before producing the little plastic recorder she had behind her back. "It's a temporary teaching tool," she explained.

"Oh, man. Is this a recorder?" He wanted to laugh but thought better of it, "I wasn't taught on one, but it took a long time for us to play real horns in class."

"This is a *real* horn!" she exclaimed. Cecilia, of course, did not think that this was true. She thought it was the most absurd thing she had ever seen. She felt ridiculous after Moe Ditham's "Barbie dream flute" remark, and she did not want to hear a similar response from her brother.

"No, I didn't mean…" Arion wasn't trying to upset her, but he could tell by her reaction that she was slightly embarrassed. "Like I said, I wasn't taught with one. Now that I think about it, I'll bet it is beneficial in the long run. You get familiar with basic concepts of sound and how to play with the rest of the band. It makes sense. I just didn't learn that way."

"Well, Mr. Hamlin says that if we work hard, we won't have to play them for very long. Believe me- I want to play the trumpet, not this lousy fairy tale prop." Cecilia waved the recorder in the air while she spoke as a way of demonstrating how truly meaningless it was to her.

"So, you're learning a scale?" Arion tried to turn his sister's attention back to what she was doing.

"I don't know," Cecilia replied honestly, "I was just following the pictures in the book."

Arion turned the book around so he could read it right side up, "Your first trumpet practice book will look similar to this one. It shows the note, and right underneath is a picture of which valves to push to make the note." He pointed to the page Cecilia had been playing from, "It looks like you were playing the B flat scale."

Cecilia blushed with excitement, "I wasn't really playing. I just did what the book said."

He continued flipping through the book, "Well, I heard someone play a scale, and you are the only person in the house with a horn in her lap." He put the book back on his sister's bed and opened it to the page with the B flat scale. "Keep practicing. After you memorize the fingerings for the notes, you should try to play the song on the next page."

Cecilia turned the page, and her eyes widened at the sight of the nameless little song. It was only one line long, but it seemed eternal to her. She flipped back and forth to the page before and noticed that the song only had notes from the B flat scale. Her brother was right again. All she had to do to play the song was learn the notes in the scale.

Arion observed his sister's reaction before asking, "You're practicing on this recorder, so that must mean you've already taken the bass clef test, right?"

Cecilia gaped at her brother and just shook her head. She wanted to play so badly that she almost forgot to study for the other test.

"Well," Arion said, "all cows eat grass."

"Excuse me, doofus, I don't have time for farm animal riddles. I have to study!" she snapped.

He took the book from her again and flipped back a few pages to the bass clef section. He quietly sat down next to his sister and simply pointed to the note on the lowest space of the staff. She turned her attention from Arion's face to where he was pointing and stared blankly at the page. The symbols were more foreign than when she first started studying for the treble clef test. Then she suddenly remembered how Arion had helped her by teaching her those mnemonic devices. Maybe he was doing the same thing now.

She thought about what Arion had said about the cows, "all cows eat grass… the first space note is A."

Arion nodded and pointed to the next space up without saying a word. "C! It's C!" Cecilia squealed.

"You've got it," He couldn't help but swell with pride at his efforts to assist his sister, "I'll tell you something about bass clef. You don't have to know it. If you're going to play the trumpet, you will only read treble clef. Just figure it out so you can get through the test. After that, you probably won't ever see it again."

Cecilia pulled the book onto her lap, "Hey, Thanks." She became so preoccupied with what Arion had just taught her that she didn't hear him slip out of her room.

***

Monday finally rolled around, and Cecilia didn't know whether to be more nervous about the test or the first recorder practice. The first half of the day soared by, so she didn't have the time to dwell on potential failure. Even lunch was exceptionally distracting because Lorelei had met a guy at the mall over the weekend. The entire half hour was filled with fantastic ramblings about her future with someone she called "the Abercrombie kid." This assured Cecilia that Lorelei had not studied for the upcoming test. On the other hand, Trilby was so overly confident about the test that it made Cecilia wonder if she was underprepared.

"Well, this is it," Trilby said as they got to the band room door, "Did you remember to bring your recorder, Lorelei?"

"Of course, I did. What kind of band student would I be if I left my instrument at home?" Lorelei asked.

Uh, the kind of student who always forgets everything and almost never studies. Cecilia thought to herself.

The three girls went into the band room and scattered to find the seat they had claimed at the end of class last time. Cecilia immediately noticed Thamyra Lirit sitting in the chair at the end of the second row. There was an empty seat next to her, but in the next seat was Lou. She quickly decided that the social sacrifice of putting herself close to Thamyra Lirit would be worth it if she got to sit next to Lou. She approached the empty seat and immediately turned her body away from Thamyra Lirit.

Thamyra Lirit hummed and hawed indiscreetly as she dug through her backpack, looking for a pencil. She pulled her recorder out and laid it on the stand, saying, "Dumb 'ol thing. I've had my own trumpet for over a year now. Why do I have to carry this kazoo around?"

Neither Cecilia nor Lou had any intention of answering Thamyra Lirit. They looked at each other and made the same annoyed face. Cecilia didn't like to make fun of people. Before she could respond verbally, Mr. Hamlin entered the room holding a stack of tests, and everybody got very quiet. He was happy that he didn't have to turn up the stereo to get their attention.

"I hope you are all ready because I sure am. Let's get this little test out of the way so we can have a real practice with your recorders," he smiled the entire time he spoke. He couldn't help it. He was excited about the big recorder practice. He couldn't wait to hear the band produce its first sound. "This test will be administered exactly like the first. Keep your test face down until I say so. When you finish, bring it to me so I can record your time. On your way back to your seat, be sure to pick up the second half of the test. Good luck, everybody."

For some reason, Cecilia wasn't as nervous about this test as she had been about the first one. She thought about each answer carefully and double-checked for errors before she looked up from the music stand she was using as a writing surface. A couple of students were already standing in front of Mr. Hamlin, turning in the first half of the test. She immediately noticed Leo, not because of his large size but because he was smiling. The boy rarely has a smile on his face. He must have been the first one finished. Cecilia smiled to herself. It made her feel good to see someone else getting into the spirit of the class.

She got in line and stood patiently behind Aki, who was tapping his pencil on the end of Mr. Hamlin's large music stand. It didn't seem to bother Mr. Hamlin as he recorded the time and gave Aki the other part of the test. Suddenly someone bumped into Cecilia's back. She spun around only to see Lou's big grinning face inches away from her. She grinned back at him and then felt an odd tapping. Aki was holding his pencil over her head and letting the eraser bounce off her hair. She craned her neck to smile at Aki and then gave Mr. Hamlin her test.

Lou and Cecilia finished the second part of the test at the same time. The rest of the class wasn't entirely done, so Cecilia sat quietly in her seat. Lou pulled a piece of paper out of his bag and drew a small tic-tac-toe board in the corner. Cecilia noticed what he was doing and got her pencil so she could play. They played a few quick games while they waited. Lou won the first two games, but Cecilia won the last one.

After the last student turned in the second half of the test, Mr. Hamlin jumped off his podium and disappeared into his office. When he returned, he had a practice book in one hand and a recorder in the other.

"Did everyone remember to bring their recorder today?" Mr. Hamlin asked with a wide, toothy smile. He placed his practice book on his stand and said, "Open your practice books to page 12. You will see a diagram of how to hold your recorder properly." He paused to let the class find the right page while he positioned his recorder in his own hands. "Just like this," he got down off of his podium and walked around to make sure everybody was holding the instrument correctly.

Cecilia felt like she knew what she was doing, but she couldn't help being nervous. Her stomach tickled, and her hands were shaking just a little bit. She sat motionless and looked as far as she could to the right to get a look at Thamyra Lirit. She was sitting still and tall, holding her recorder. Cecilia looked as far as she could to the left and saw Lou sitting up with his recorder as well. Neither of them looked as nervous as Cecilia. They both seemed quite sure of themselves. She took this to mean that there was nothing to be nervous about and tried to relax.

Mr. Hamlin returned to his podium and instructed the class to turn the page, "This is your first scale. Someone tell me which scale this is." Mr. Hamlin was overwhelmed at how many hands were in the air. He could tell that this was going to be a great class. He had almost learned everybody's name but the sight of all the eager hands took him by surprise. He pointed into the sea of hands, saying, "Uh... uh ... blue shirt...uh," he glanced down at his roll book to jog his memory, "Um... Soni!" He wasn't sure if he got the name right, but the student he was pointing to was the one that answered.

"B flat," Soni replied with much confidence.

"Correct," Mr. Hamlin began thinking that the class was probably just as excited as he was about today's practice. "Great, I see some of you had a chance to open your practice books this weekend. Let's see if we can make sound." He stepped off the podium again, "Make sure that your fingers are in the same position as the diagram under the note. Now put your mouth around the mouthpiece like this, but please don't blow yet." He turned sideways so everyone could see what he was doing, and then he looked around the room again to make sure everyone held the mouthpiece correctly in their mouth. He could tell by looking at someone if they were doing it wrong. When done correctly, a person playing a recorder is forced to make a distinctive and ridiculous face. Everybody in the class was making the facial expression Mr. Hamlin was looking for.

This time when he stepped onto the podium, he put his recorder down on his stool and put his hands in the air. Something extraordinary was about to happen. When his hands came down, the whole class would blow a light stream of air through their recorder and make its first bit of sound, real musical sound. Cecilia looked around at the class, and all the humiliation from carrying around the recorder melted away. Everyone in class was doing the same thing at the same time, so no one looked dumber than the other. She would have smiled if she didn't have to keep her mouth positioned around her recorder.

"Now, when I bring my hands up like this, you will all breath in," Mr. Hamlin demonstrated his arm movements slowly as he spoke. "And when I bring my hands back down near the podium like this, you will breathe out and into the mouthpiece of the recorder." He glanced around the room to make sure that everybody was prepared to follow his directions when suddenly his eyes stopped, and his arms fell. The whole class turned their attention to where Mr. Hamlin was staring. Mr. Alvis, the assistant director of the high school marching band, had snuck into the band room. He was leaning against the frame of the door with his arms crossed and a sly smile on his face.

"Sorry I'm late," he said without moving from the doorway.

"Mr. Alvis! Oh, I almost forgot you were coming. I still get so excited when the students first learn to play," Mr. Hamlin approached Mr. Alvis with his hand extended in preparation for a vigorous handshake. "Goodness, my percussion players probably thought I had forgotten all about them." He made his way toward the back of the room and began moving the drums out the door. "Help out, guys. Would you two push the bass, and Aki can grab the snare? Everybody else can round up all the drumsticks and mallets."

As soon as Mr. Alvis and Mr. Hamlin had left the room, a low mumble of conversation began. Cecilia and Lou immediately looked at each other and began talking, but neither heard a word the other said because they both spoke very quickly and at the same time.

Some students played their recorders very softly, but none of them were playing the scale. They were playing simply because they could. Cecilia was comforted by the low hum of all the little conversations and the random interjection of a musical note here and there. It filled her with the kind of warmth that reminded her of family visiting during the holidays or friends at a birthday party. She knew that she was where she belonged and that she wouldn't have to be the best trumpet player in the world to have fun in band. It wasn't long before Mr. Hamlin came jogging back into the room and onto his podium.

"Let's try all that again," He put his hands in the air again and made sure everybody was still ready to play, "Make sure your fingers are covering the correct holes. We are playing the first note on the page."

Mr. Hamlin raised his arms, and the whole class followed his directions precisely and took a breath in. He almost shook with excitement as he lowered his hands closer to the podium.

Cecilia was trembling when she saw Mr. Hamlin's hands in the air. She tried to play it cool like Lou, but she couldn't hide the quivering horn in her hands. Everything stopped when she played. When the air came out of her mouth, all she could hear was the note. She kept her eyes on Mr. Hamlin's hands and her ears tuned in to the wonderful sound she and her classmates were making. It felt as if the entire world came to life to celebrate this glorious musical moment.

Mr. Hamlin held up his hands as if he were suspending the note in the air right before their eyes. He slowly moved his hands in a circle to cut the note off. As he closed his hands, the class stopped breathing into their recorders, and the room was silent again.

Mr. Hamlin beamed with pride, "That was wonderful. A little out of tune, but we are here to work on that. Let's go slow and play each note in the scale. Keep your eyes on my hands so you know when to change notes."

Cecilia fixed her eyes on Mr. Hamlin's hands. She was ready to play again. She didn't know what "out of tune" meant, and she didn't care. She was fascinated at how a room full of middle school students could cooperate and create such perfection, out of tune or not. She wasn't nervous anymore. This time when Mr. Hamlin put his hands up, she did not shake, and her horn did not tremble. He clarified that they would play the next note in the scale, so Cecilia checked to make sure her fingers were in the right place.

"Hands up, breathe in—hands down, breathe out and play," Mr. Hamlin spoke as he gestured accordingly. He reeled at the sound of his beginner band playing their first scale. He tried to remain composed, but he could not stop his pride from plastering a smile on his face.

Everyone looked around the room in amazement. They were all very impressed with themselves. Mr. Hamlin gave them a brief moment to let the experience sink in before moving on with more instruction.

"This is just wonderful," he couldn't help but say. "Let's try the arpeggio. Who remembers what an arpeggio is?"

Of course, Thamyra Lirit was the first one to have her hand in the air. Lou and Cecilia looked at one another and silently rolled their eyes in contempt.

"It is when you play the first, third, and fifth notes of the scale," Thamyra answered knowingly.

"Very good, Thamyra," responded Mr. Hamlin. "Everyone take your pencil and mark the first, third, and fifth notes of this scale." He waited for everyone to do as he asked and then put his baton in the air. "You should be ready to play when my hands are in the air like this."

Cecilia was still marking the fifth note of the scale when she heard Mr. Hamlin. She quickly dropped her pencil and put her recorder to her lips. Mr. Hamlin slowly conducted them through each note of the arpeggio. He used the fingers on the hand that wasn't holding the baton to remind the class which note was next. The transitions between the notes were rather clumsy. It took everyone a second to consult the practice book and change fingering for each note. Mr. Hamlin was proud all the same. He knew that they would all turn out to be fine musicians with his encouragement and a little practice.

"We will play this scale and its arpeggio as a warm-up every day," he began. "Hopefully, you will commit it to memory after playing it so often. Also, be sure to practice this and the other scales in your everyday practice at home. This is important because it will help you prepare for your playing test."

Mr. Hamlin paused for effect before continuing, "A playing test is where you prove what you have learned by playing for me. I'll set up a video camera in my office, and you will each take turns one by one. You will play one scale and arpeggio from memory, and you cannot play the warm-up scale. Then, using your practice books, play one of the three songs I will give you beforehand. It will be any of the songs in your practice books we play in class. Everyone must pass the playing test in order for us to switch to real instruments." He took a breath to finish what he was saying, but the bell rang and interrupted him.

"Darn it," Mr. Hamlin grumbled as he looked down at his watch as if it were the fault of time itself that class ended so abruptly rather than his forgetfulness. "All right, hold your questions until tomorrow, and we will start where we left off."

Lou, Cecilia, Lorelei, and Trilby all hurriedly packed up their things so they could talk for a second before their next class. Trilby ran right up to Cecilia, but she didn't get a chance to speak because Lorelei came up behind her and squawked her horn as loud as she could. The room got quiet for a second, and everyone turned their attention to where the noise was coming from. They looked around at all the eyes on them but then looked back at each other and laughed.

"Cecilia, are you coming?" Caroline yelled from the band room door. She had to stick her head in against the flow of students exiting the room to get Cecilia's attention.

"Oh, man. We're going to be late," Trilby said, looking up at the big clock over Mr. Hamlin's office door.

Cecilia caught up with Caroline, and they made their way to exploratory hall. Caroline kept a quick pace so they would make it to home economis on time. "We made it," she said as they stepped through the door.

"Sorry I almost made us late," Cecilia apologized.

"Don't worry about it. Besides, the quicker we get down the hall, the less chance we have of running into those gross Ditham boys," Caroline winced when she spoke of Ben and Moe. "Anyway, I would leave you to walk by yourself if I thought you would make me late."

"Thanks, pal," Cecilia managed to say with a smile as Mrs. Shannon began instructing the class how to thread a sewing machine properly.

Chapter Six

Band became Cecilia's favorite class. It lasted the same amount of time as any other class on her schedule, but somehow it felt like the shortest class of the day. She carried her recorder with a new sense of pride rather than shame and embarrassment. Trilby and Lorelei were also enjoying band. After hearing Thamyra Lirit go on and on about how she knows everything, Trilby suggested that they have practice at each other's house after school a couple of times a week.

Trilby was serious about practice. Cecilia knew it was because she was so good at it. She loved playing scales over and over again, playing the notes faster each time. Lorelei spent most of her time making jokes and finding ways to create the most annoying squawks and squeaks with her recorder. Cecilia would never consider excluding Lorelei from after-school practice because she was her dear friend, and her mother made the absolute best snacks. One time the girls got off the bus at Lorelei's house just when Mrs. Besset was taking some of her blue-ribbon banana-nut bread out of the oven. She even served it to them while it was still warm. Lou never missed a day of school, so naturally, he never missed an after-school practice. He always kept them on task and did a good job keeping time when they practiced playing the songs.

One Friday afternoon, the four of them gathered in front of the school to wait for Arion to pick them up and take them to Cecilia's house for their last after-school practice before the playing test.

"Why is your brother picking us up? Doesn't he have practice or something?" Lorelei asked as she swayed back and forth impatiently.

"Home game tonight. He just has to be back at the high school by five. Mom will be home from work before he has to leave," Cecilia explained.

Trilby reached for her book bag and said, "Here he comes."

Arion didn't get out of the car. Lorelei, Trilby, and Cecilia jumped in the back seat so fast that Lou had no choice but to sit up front with Arion. The radio was so loud that nobody could hear each other talk, so they sat silently during the short ride. The minute they got to the house, Cecilia and her friends hopped out of the car and ran inside.

"Let's put our stuff in my room and then come back down for a snack," Cecilia suggested.

Lorelei ran up the stairs hollering something about having to use the bathroom. Cecilia laughed and followed Trilby and Lou up toward her bedroom. Lorelei didn't quite get her things into Cecilia's room, so Trilby and Cecilia each grabbed a strap of her book bag and dragged it into the room. Trilby let go before Cecilia, and the weight of the heavy bag yanked her arm down toward the floor. She looked up so she could tell Trilby that she was about as much help as Lorelei, but she froze and let go of the book bag strap.

Lorelei quickly returned to Cecilia's room and immediately began running her mouth, "Hey, thanks for bringing my stuff in. You know I have homework in every subject this weekend. I swear that math teacher thinks his is the only class on my schedule. I can't spend all weekend on just one subject, but you should see the handouts he gave us. ALL word problems!" She finally stopped talking and noticed that nobody was listening to her. They were standing in the middle of the room with their mouths hanging open, staring at the bed. Trilby followed the path of their gaze to what looked like a small trunk or suitcase on Cecilia's bed. "Hey, are you going on a trip or something?"

"Shhh," Trilby said softly.

"What?" Lorelei was confused and didn't know why her friends had suddenly become catatonic. "I don't hear anything."

Trilby stopped staring long enough to look at Lorelei disapprovingly. She raised her arm and pointed to the mysterious case on Cecilia's bed, "Open your eyes. That's no suitcase." Lorelei looked back at the case and wrinkled her forehead. She still didn't get it.

Trilby looked into Cecilia's eyes. She hadn't blinked once. Trilby waved her hand slowly in Cecilia's line of sight. Cecilia gently moved the obstruction from her view and walked toward the bed.

She touched the case with just her index finger and felt the smooth texture of the leather. It was old, brown, and beautiful. She ran her finger along the edge of the case. Of course, she wasn't entirely convinced it was a trumpet case. So what if it was? Who said that there would be anything in it? She put her hands on each clasp and gradually flipped them one at a time. She closed her eyes as she opened the case. The hinges were well-greased, so the top flopped right down on the bed. She heard one of her friends gasp. She took a deep breath and opened her eyes.

There it was. A brass-plated trumpet shining like a treasure. Cecilia's treasure. She couldn't speak. She felt her friends step closer for a better look. It was the greatest moment of her short life. Her future was staring her in the face. She was going to be good at something.

"Can I talk now?" Lorelei decided that she should be the one to break the silence. "What's the big deal? You knew you would get a horn someday. You *are* in band class."

"Just let me enjoy this moment, Lorelei. Living with my perfect brother gives me little opportunity to experience glory like this," Cecilia spoke very calmly.

She couldn't take her eyes off the trumpet. Her hand made its way from the clasp to the fuzzy lining of the case. She was afraid that the trumpet would disappear if she tried to touch it. Leaning in for a closer look, she saw her distorted reflection in the bell of the horn. She stared unblinking while she worked up the courage to touch the cold, golden metal.

Trilby stood behind Cecilia with her hands over her mouth in disbelief. She knew she was getting a hand-me-down flute from her cousin, who was never very serious about playing it. Trilby didn't care where it came from or who had it first. She just wanted to play. But she was sure Cecilia wasn't expecting to find a trumpet on her bed when she came home from school that day. She was irritated with the way Lorelei was handling the situation. She could be insensitive at times. It didn't seem to bother Cecilia. Nothing could. She was completely mesmerized.

"Do you guys see this?" Cecilia finally managed to say.

"Uh, you mean the big shiny thing you've been staring at?" Lorelei couldn't help but be sarcastic. She thought stupid questions deserved even stupider answers.

"Congratulations," Lou said in an attempt to counter Lorelei's casual attitude.

"I had no idea … I mean … um…I," Cecilia began to stammer.

"Take a breath," Trilby said.

"Yes, take several," Lou recommended.

"Are we going to stand here all day?" Lorelei asked impatiently.

"Don't tell me that you are in a hurry to practice your recorder," Trilby replied.

Lorelei considered her options and decided to stand in silent protest instead of complaining and ruining the moment.

"How did this get here?" Cecilia asked as she slowly took the horn out of its case. She knew she wasn't holding it correctly, but she just had to pick it up and inspect every shiny inch to make sure it was real. She looked each of her friends in the eye to ensure they were looking at what was in her hands. Lorelei was ready to blurt out another sarcastic comment, but her better judgment stopped her before she could open her mouth.

"I can answer that," Arion's voice broke the spell they were under. All four of them turned their attention from the horn to the door. He looked right at Cecilia and continued, "It used to belong to a friend of mine. You remember, everyone used to call him Bubba Jon. He was one of the best players on the team, and this year he's off playing football at college. I happened to mention your interest in playing trumpet in band, so he left his horn at home. His mom gave dad a good deal." He paused and waited for her to say something, but she just stared back at him blankly. "You need some oil for the valves and a new mouthpiece, but we can get those things at MacArthur's Music Store."

Cecilia couldn't believe her ears. Her brother was being nice. He had done something for her, "Thank you."

Arion smiled back at her, "Your welcome."

"You've been my brother my whole life, and you have never done anything for me out of the goodness of your heart," Cecilia couldn't help but be both grateful and suspicious.

"You're right. I want something. But it is simple, and you might have fun," Arion replied.

"Oh, man!" It didn't take long for the light bulb to come on in Cecilia's head, "You want me to go to a football game, don't you?" Cecilia hated football. She didn't get it. She couldn't follow the game, all those penalties and positions. Arion tried to explain it to her, but she never got interested in the game.

Arion's smile widened, "Just one. Come on. Home game tonight. You'll get to see the marching band perform during halftime."

Lou looked at Cecilia, "It is a small price to pay for such a generous gesture."

Cecilia glared back at him, "Thank you, Lou. Maybe you would like to come with me this evening."

"Oh, me too!" Trilby shouted. "I love sitting in the student section with my sisters. They never miss a game."

Cecilia looked at Lorelei. "If everybody else is going, I guess I'll go too," She mumbled.

"You win. It looks like we're going to the game tonight," Cecilia said to her brother. "I like the trumpet. That was pretty cool of you. But this is it. I'm only going to this one game. Deal?"

"One game," Arion agreed and walked away from his sister's room with a feeling of satisfaction he had never felt before, even on the football field.

"I can't believe we have to practice our recorders after this. How am I going to concentrate with this horn on my bed and the stupid game to go to," Cecilia searched her friends' faces for sympathy. Not even Lorelei could agree with her aversion to practice because she was the one who needed it the most. They all got their recorders and practice books and headed for the den.

By now, they had committed the everyday warm-up routine to memory. Lou tapped his foot loudly to keep the beat and gestured slightly with his horn to make sure everyone began and ended at the same time. It was a brief practice due to Cecilia's indifference and Lorelei's impatience. They got through several scales and a couple of songs. Cecilia was reminded of Arion's earlier comment about playing the same song over and over. At least she wasn't playing alone.

***

Friday night high school football was a big deal in Brementon, especially since there was nothing else to do in town. Cecilia could sense where she was even if her mother drove around in circles and she wore a blindfold. She smelled the stadium grass before they even got settled into a parking space. It was as if it had been cut minutes before they arrived. After everybody got out of the car, she got a good whiff of the greasy junk food waiting for them at the concession stand. Each step they took brought them closer to the crowd and the overwhelming murmur generated by that many people all talking at the same time.

"Wait up," squeaked Trilby from behind them. She couldn't keep up with the group since she was wearing what looked like the most uncomfortable shoes in the world.

"Why did you wear that outfit and those shoes? You look like you're going to a club or something," Lorelei mumbled as they all turned around and waited for their overdressed friend. "Leave it to you to sacrifice comfort for fashion. These are the most comfortable overalls in the world, and I always wear them to games." She motioned to her own outfit and gave a little curtsy.

Cecilia looked down at her clothes. She wore blue jeans and an old BHS football t-shirt she got from her brother. Since she was thinking about it, she looked at what Lou was wearing, too. He looked like he had just stepped out of a catalog with his neatly pressed khaki shorts and striped golf shirt. She had to agree with Lorelei's earlier statement about comfort. She wouldn't be able to enjoy herself if she was teetering around like Trilby or worrying about getting some random stain or wrinkle on Lou's khaki shorts.

"When we get to our seats, you won't have to worry about it because we will be sitting down watching the game." Cecilia's mom was the voice of reason above the strange fashion debate keeping them from the stadium gate. "Your father and I brought the camera to take pictures of your brother while he's playing tonight. Let's pick up the pace so we can get a good seat on the fifty-yard line."

"No offense Mrs. Banbury but I was going to sit in the student section." Lou had no intention of sitting next to Arion's #1 fans and listening to them go on and on about how great he plays. That was one thing Cecilia, and he always agreed on, her parents were strangely fixated on their son's athleticism, and they weren't afraid to show it.

"Mom, we want to sit with our friends," Cecilia pleaded.

Mr. Banbury caught up with them just in time to hear what Cecilia said. "I get it. Your mother and I drive you out here, and you leave us high and dry."

"Come on, dad. You know I don't want to hear you tell everyone seated around us that your son is 'magic on the football field' and that 'nobody can stop him once he gets a hold of that ball.'" Cecilia said in a mocking tone.

Mrs. Banbury laughed to herself. She thought Cecilia sounded exactly like her father. She also knew Cecilia was making fun of her a little bit, too, since she was guilty of the same thing. She had millions of pictures of Arion on the field. She looked at all the kids and then back at her husband, "Let's go, hon. They'll meet us at the car after the game." She turned back to Cecilia and her friends, "Try to get here on time despite Trilby's shoe problems."

"Yay!" Lorelei hollered. She had hoped they wouldn't have to sit with the adults all night. Sitting in the student section was the most fun.

Cecilia's parents hurried off in search of the perfect seat, and she looked at Trilby, "Seriously, piggyback on Lou or something. At this rate, we won't get there by half-time."

"I'm not carrying anybody." Lou quickly stated in protest. "Just carry the stupid shoes until we get into the stadium."

Trilby couldn't decide if she was more frustrated with the shoes or her friends. No wonder her sister gave them to her. They must have been hard for her to walk in too. She took the shoes off and picked up the pace. By the time she got them back on, the crowd was so thick that everybody was walking just as slow as she was.

Cecilia had never sat in the student section before, but she knew where it was. Everybody did because that's where most of the noise and cheering came from. She stayed in line behind Lou and followed her friends through the crowd. She caught sight of her parents for a second and quickly waved, thinking to herself how they had picked a good spot to take pictures. Maybe one day, they would be fighting their way into the stadium to see her march. She imagined all the things they would say while they bragged about how their daughter would be the star of the half-time show. Mom would wave like she always does at Arion, even though he is playing and can't wave back. She always waves.

Cecilia looked up and noticed Lou was no longer standing in front of her. She looked right and saw the football players warming up for the game. She looked left and saw the mighty staircase that led straight up to the student section. As she began the climb to the top, she remembered the other reason the student section was such a good place for her to sit. It was right next to the band. On the other side of the stairs was the entire Brementon High School marching band in full uniform and ready to put on a show. She even recognized some of the people who had come to her school to talk about their instruments. She got goosebumps just thinking about sitting in the band section in one of those uniforms.

It was easy to find her friends in the thick mob of people because Trilby was exceptionally tall in her unfortunately uncomfortable shoes, easy to spot in a crowd. Lou saved Cecilia a spot. Everyone was standing on the bleachers.

"Isn't this great! We get to sit right next to the band!" Lorelei yelled as she popped up in between Lou and Cecilia.

Cecilia asked, "Oh, now you're Mrs. Band, huh?"

"I have a perfect view of that drummer from here. Remember the one who came to class that time?" Lorelei explained, but Cecilia knew who she was talking about.

Suddenly Cecilia noticed that the band members were shifting in their seats in preparation for something, and the football team had left the field. She looked at Lou and smiled wide. The cheerleaders came bounding out onto the field and held up the ceremonial paper banner for the football team to run through.

The band director did not stand to direct the band. Cecilia looked down at the drum major with curiosity and wondered if the whole band really would take direction from one of their own. Just a student. He lifted his arms, and the band was on its feet with their horns in the air. He counted it off and the whole band began playing the fight song. Sitting that close, Cecilia thought she could literally feel each note. She could definitely feel the beat of the drums. The football team ran around and burst through the paper obstruction the cheerleaders had spent all week preparing for just this moment.

Unusual tradition. Cecilia thought to herself. Everyone clapped and cheered, and the game began. Other than being with her friends, Cecilia quickly lost interest in the game. "I think I'll head down and get a hot dog or something."

Lou could tell she was bored, and he tried to explain that they were about to score a touchdown. She could care less, and he knew it. However, the energy in the stadium was slowly rising the closer the Brementon High Lions got to the end zone. The drum major was on his feet. Lou looked at Cecilia and noticed she was paying more attention to the band than the game.

The band began playing again, but it wasn't the fight song. It was something else, but everybody else seemed to know it because they were clapping and singing along. Some of the older boys danced in the aisles and imitated the cheerleaders' routine. Lou was sure Cecilia wouldn't be leaving to get that hot dog any time soon. The band kept her captivated for the majority of the game.

The Lions were winning. The band played the fight song several times. But before the second quarter was half over, the band and the flag corps slowly filed out of the stands. Cecilia's heart sank.

Lou saw her expression change. "Half-time show," he reminded her.

Her smile widened, and she became antsy with anticipation. She was jumpier and louder than Lorelei ever could have been. Lou laughed to himself. He had no idea Cecilia had been that worked up and excited about band. She glared at the clock. She watched it wind down to zero, ending the first half.

"Thank goodness. I'm starving. Let's get a snack," Trilby suggested as she made her way past her friends.

"Are you crazy? The band is about to play," Cecilia pointed out.

"I hate to point this out," noted Lorelei, "But they have been playing off and on all during the first half." She couldn't help being sarcastic since they were sitting next to the band the whole time.

"Well, I hate football," Cecilia explained, "I came to see this."

The band hit the field just as soon as the football players were off it. Most people were making their way to the concession stand, so she had a clear view of the entire band. The drum major stood on a huge box on the fifty-yard line. He lifted his arms, and the band was in motion. It was mesmerizing how they moved around and made designs, circles, and straight lines while playing instruments. The instruments sparkled under the stadium lights as they twirled around like fireflies celebrating the night.

Sometimes a colorful flag would catch Cecilia's eye, but she was more focused on the band than the flag corps. She watched the drum major conduct his band, his friends, his classmates. She watched the trumpet players hold their brassy horns high and spray melody and sound throughout the audience. They all marched on the same foot at the same time and did almost the same thing. She was in absolute awe and could picture herself in the middle of all of it. She could see herself on that football field with her friends marching and her parents watching intently.

A sudden and thunderous drum roll brought her eye back - the fight song again. Everyone was on their feet, and the band made a massive star around the drum line. The cheering didn't stop until the band left the field.

Cecilia looked at her friends and smiled, "Okay, who's hungry?"

"I was about 10 minutes ago," Lorelei snapped. She can get cranky sometimes when she hasn't eaten in a while. "Maybe there won't a line since we waited so long."

Trilby grabbed Cecilia's hand for balance and tottered slowly down the stairs. She didn't mind. She was still thinking about the band. She supported Trilby as Lou and Lorelei raced toward the food they had waited so long for. By the time they waddled up to the food line, Lou was stuffing a huge slice of pizza in his mouth, and Lorelei was pouring ketchup and mustard over a couple of hot dogs. Lorelei was right. The line was shorter since everyone was watching the game.

The rest of the game fascinated Cecilia as much as it had from the start. She was filled with excitement and was looking forward to the future. She had never felt that before and didn't want the feeling to go away. She hoped the novelty of it would never wear off.

Everyone helped Trilby back to the car. Lorelei carried the shoes, and Lou and Cecilia each stood on one side of her and helped her walk. "I'm giving my sister her shoes back the minute I get home," she grumbled.

Chapter Seven

After the football game, Cecilia thought about band class differently than before. She couldn't see the obstacles anymore. She wasn't afraid of having to practice. She wanted to march. She kept playing the half-time show in her head like a movie over and over. She was so focused on her ultimate goal that the tasks at hand seemed petty and simple compared to what she had to look forward to.

She hadn't touched her new trumpet again after she got it. She kept thinking that it would disappear or that she would have to give it back. She locked it away in its case right next to her closet door. That way, it will be right there on the day she gets to take it to school. She would put her book bag over her shoulder, grab the trumpet case by its worn leather handle, and proudly step out of her room. Until then, she made a silent wish every day that it would not disappear and that it would always be hers, just in case.

She spent the rest of the weekend diligently rehearsing her scales and thumbing through her practice book. They had played several songs in class, and she had even memorized one. She quickly realized that Mr. Hamlin had been right about remembering the songs and scales they play every day. She confidently played the B flat scale and its arpeggio without looking at the fingering chart in her book. She wanted to do well. In truth, she wanted everyone to do well. Mr. Hamlin told them that everyone had to pass the playing test on recorders before they could play their instruments. Cecilia imagined each one of her classmates sitting just like she was in a quiet room practicing.

Monday morning, she was still confident and hopped down the stairs for breakfast like it was a great day already. She dug right into the waffles on the counter and looked around for some bacon.

"Ready for your big test today?" Her mother had been in the room the whole time but didn't speak until Cecilia's mouth was full.

She swallowed hard and asked, "What test?" between bites.

"I pay more attention than you know. Besides, you've been playing that recorder all weekend. Your playing test is today, right?" Sometimes her mother seemed to know everything.

"I'm ready. I've been practicing with Lou and them after school for weeks now. I sat right down and practiced just like we did in class. I should do okay." Cecilia replied coolly.

Arion had come into the kitchen by now, "Talking about the playing test, huh?"

"I was just saying how prepared I am," she said.

"No pressure either," Arion explained, "You're in a room with a video camera. Just pretend you're practicing in your room. Nobody but you and Mr. Hamlin will know what happens during that test."

"What don't you two understand? I'm prepared. I've been practicing. I am not nervous, but I will be if we keep talking about it like this!" Cecilia hoped she had made her point and was anxious for the subject to change.

"She's right," their mother said. "Get your things together and get going before you're both late for school."

Arion didn't say anything in the car. He was excited for her when he found out she wanted to play the trumpet. Watching her study and listening to her practice reminded him of when he first learned to play. He was horrible. Everyone in his class was in the beginning, but they learned and grew together until they could play beautiful music in concert. He knew precisely what Cecilia was going through, and he couldn't help but feel the anticipation along with her.

"Hey," Cecilia finally decided to start a conversation, "When you were in band, was it like the shortest class of the day? I mean, because you're playing your horn, so it's not like you're really in school. It … it's like, um." As she trailed off, Arion jumped right in to finish her sentence.

"It's fun, isn't it." He turned his attention away from the road for a second to smile at her, "It doesn't make you a geek. If it does, that means that all those other people are geeks too. Band geeks. The ones in band now, and the ones that were in band. It would mean that I am a band geek because band has always been my favorite class. That's why I've always made room for it in my schedule, even though I play football in the fall. Trust me, they all enjoy it as much, if not more than you do."

She smiled and thanked him for the ride as she stepped out of the car in front of the school. She was quite sure of herself. The fact that her brother knew exactly how she felt gave her an extra boost of confidence that she wasn't expecting. They all want to be good at something, just like she does. They all enjoy class just like she does. They all look forward to the next day, the next lesson, and the next new song.

When Cecilia got to homeroom, she noticed that Lorelei wasn't there yet. She knew that Lorelei hadn't taken band very seriously and wondered if she would even show up for school. She tried to focus on Mrs. Tallbay as she made a few start-of-week announcements, but she kept turning in her seat to see if Lorelei was coming down the hall. It wouldn't have been the first time Lorelei was conveniently ill on the same day as a test, but this was different. It wasn't any old test. The grade mattered to the whole class. When they got their recorders, Mr. Hamlin said everybody had to pass. It was burned into Cecilia's brain because she worried about relying so heavily on each classmate's ability to do well on the playing test. The bell rang, and she made her way to Mr. Duke's class for science. She glanced up the hallway one more time, hoping to see Lorelei darting to class but wound up in first period without seeing her.

Mr. Duke rearranged the whole classroom for a particular experiment he wanted to do. Cecilia was delighted to have something to distract her from the playing test and Lorelei's attendance. Unfortunately, the rest of the day oozed by like ketchup making its way out of a glass bottle.

History was her second period class, and Mr. Frode was anything but interesting, although he thought he was brilliant. He would tell jokes that nobody else in the class would laugh at, but he would still chuckle to himself. Today it was like he knew how anxious Cecilia was. She kept thinking he was trying extra hard to be as dull and long-winded as possible. She wasn't squirming in her seat or tapping her foot, but something about her face showed the world that she was uneasy about something. The longer and duller the day got, the more she became uncomfortable and slowly lost the confidence she woke up with.

When it was finally time for English class, Cecilia's anxiety melted when she saw both Trilby and Lorelei saving a seat for her in class. It was like the anxiety of the morning was wasted energy that she could have used to focus on class. (Especially since she practically missed everything Ms. Bilge had to say about fractions. Cecilia was terrible with fractions. She knew if she studied with Lou this week, he would help her out. He was good at everything.)

So, she skipped across the room to the desk between her friends and immediately asked Lorelei, "Where were you this morning? I thought you were ditching so you wouldn't have to take the playing test."

"Why would you think that?" Lorelei seemed a little offended. "Like I don't know how to prepare for a test. I don't study, do my homework or practice. Is that it?"

Trilby couldn't help but put her two cents in at this point, "Uh, yea. You've avoided homework ever since elementary school. Don't act like we don't know you. You pretended to have the flu to get out of the science fair last year because you never even came up with an experiment to present. Remember?"

"Okay," Lorelei couldn't deny what Trilby had said, "I want to stay in band. You have to play if you want to stay, right? So, I spent the day yesterday reviewing and practicing scales, arpeggios, and songs."

"Well, good," Cecilia smiled with relief. Maybe today would be a good day for everybody.

The three girls stopped talking just as Mrs. Tallbay began discussing how to diagram a sentence. Cecilia spent the rest of the class period happily working on grammar and not thinking about the playing test for the first time all day.

For the first time all year, they walked to band class in complete silence. There was a bit of tension in the air that couldn't be broken by conversation. Cecilia turned to Lorelei and Trilby before she opened the door, "Ready?" They both simply nodded in response.

When the door came open, a rush of random honks, squeaks, scales, and songs filled the tiny hallway. Anyone who had made it to class by now was already preparing. All of the girls in the front row, who will soon be playing flutes, were gathered in a tight semi-circle playing scales together. Trilby quickly grabbed her recorder from her bag and joined them.

Cecilia and Lorelei also found their way to their respective sections. Most people were silently reviewing fingering charts, but some had grouped or paired up to practice songs and scales together. Cecilia liked practicing with someone else. It made her feel less self-conscience about making mistakes. Lou was seated in his usual seat, and Cecilia took her place next to him. He was playing when she first sat down, but he stopped to show her where he was in the practice book.

"Want to play along?" Lou asked cheerfully. He knew Cecilia was still timid about playing by herself. She smiled in silent response and put her horn to her lips. Lou tapped his foot to set the tempo, and together they played the scale and arpeggio on the page.

It wasn't long before Mr. Hamlin came into the room. He intentionally waited in the chorus room until just before the bell rang. If he wasn't standing over everyone, they were more likely to practice and experiment with their horns. He liked the sound of a room full of motivated students taking the initiative to play and prepare on their own. Sure enough, when he walked in, the whole class was focused on their practice books, reviewing fingering charts, and playing some scales and songs. Some students were practicing together, but everyone was playing something different. It was a magical dissonance that Mr. Hamlin considered the greatest sound in the world.

Some students stopped playing when they saw Mr. Hamlin come in, although he did not instruct them to do so. He was smiling and looking around the room at all the talented faces that he had such high hopes for. He could tell they were nervous. The tardy bell rang, but everyone had already been in their seats for quite a while. By now, they had stopped playing and were looking at Mr. Hamlin, silently awaiting instruction.

Cecilia looked around at her classmates and noticed that everyone had not only fallen silent, but they all looked just as stressed as she felt. For some reason, this made her feel better.

"You all look like you're waiting to be executed," Mr. Hamlin finally broke the ice, and a few people giggled. Nervous laughter. "So, we are all going to warm-up together. We have this down to a real routine by now. How should we begin?"

Everyone looked around at each other in confusion. Nobody could tell if he was really asking or if it was a rhetorical question. Of course, Thamyra Lirit was there to announce the answer like some great proclamation, "B flat scale and arpeggio." Right out loud without raising her hand. At least it broke the bizarre silence that had developed and was somehow echoing through the room.

"Let's get going then," Mr. Hamlin was as anxious to give the playing test as the students were ready to get it over with. "Hands up, horns up."

Practice began just like it did every other day, which gave Cecilia a piece of her confidence back. Everyone was doing what they usually do. The drummers were playing along to the beat Mr. Hamlin maintained like a human metronome. That whole few minutes of class brought everyone together and reminded each of them that they were fully capable of completing a simple playing test.

Because it began like any other day, the class was comforted but it was quickly broken when Mr. Hamlin said, "Now, it's time to begin the playing test."

After hearing this, Trilby, Lorelei, Cecilia, and Lou all looked around at one another. Each of them shared the same frightened expression of anticipation on their faces. Cecilia looked out the corner of her eye at Thamyra Lirit and was not surprised to see a fearless and overly prepared student ready to take a test. She suddenly felt bad that Thamyra didn't have anyone to share her glory and certainty with.

Mr. Hamlin couldn't remember a time when this particular class was so silent and attentive. Every eye in the room was on his face, and every ear was tuned to his voice.

"Let's talk about how this works. Each of you will go into my office one at a time. There is a clipboard on the desk. Make sure you record your name and the scale and song you have decided to play. When you begin playing, take your time. You may start over if you like. Try not to take too long because everybody needs a turn. This could take until tomorrow, so don't feel rushed."

He looked around the room to make sure he still had their attention. None of them had blinked since he began talking, "Remember, you must play the scale and arpeggio from memory, but you may use your book to play the song. We will continue to have practice, so try to move around carefully and quietly."

Cecilia noticed that even Lou was beginning to tense up. This was an important moment, and she could tell everyone else in the room was equally anxious. She looked up at Lorelei, who had been seeking an affirming smile from a friend. Trilby sat tall and hung on every word Mr. Hamlin said. She was sitting so close that Cecilia thought she might join him on the podium. She quickly turned her attention back to Mr. Hamlin as he gave further instructions.

"Okay, one at a time, I will take volunteers to go into my office and play. Those of you who wish to wait will be called in alphabetical order by last name. Don't forget to write your name and announce yourself to the camera."

Cecilia's heart sank. Her last name began with a B. She was going to be one of the first to go unless the whole class volunteered to play before her. Judging by the tension in the room, she doubted that that would happen. She suddenly noticed Thamyra Lirit had changed positions in her chair. She was sitting on the edge of her seat with her hand thrust into the air. The statue of liberty would have a hard time competing with Thamyra's current posture and pride.

"Ah, Miss Lirit. Do you have a question, or are you volunteering to play first?" Mr. Hamlin asked.

"I'm ready to play," she responded like some kind of soldier accepting a mission.

"Fantastic! Make sure you sit in front of the camera and do not adjust the chair or the camera in any way," He explained, "announce yourself and write your name on the clipboard."

Without batting an eye, Thamyra Lirit jumped out of her seat and went right into Mr. Hamlin's office. She looked fearless. Cecilia wondered if any of her friends would be that brave. Lou was smart and always good to practice with. Surely, he would volunteer to play.

"Back to class," Mr. Hamlin drew everyone's attention away from the office door, "We usually all play the same thing, and each of you plays the same notes in the same key. When you learn to play your instruments, each section will play a different melody, and you will not always play the same thing as the person next to you." He walked away from the podium toward the small piano up against the sidewall. He stood in front of the keys and played "Mary had a Little Lamb" one note at a time. "What is it called when the entire band plays the same thing all together?"

There was a brief pause before anyone dared to guess an answer. Lou looked around the room and then began thumbing through his practice book. Cecilia looked at him and then back at Mr. Hamlin.

"Yes, look it up," Mr. Hamlin encouraged, "If you don't know the answer, use your resources to find it."

Cecilia didn't know where to begin to look. They had only practiced a few key pages of the book, and she wasn't sure which one to flip to. Where do I look for new words? She suddenly remembered a moment in her history class from earlier that day. There was a boldface word she didn't recognize, so she used the glossary at the end of the book to get the definition. So instead of turning to the first page, or any other page she had read from before, she turned to the very back page. She was so excited to have found it that she almost forgot to raise her hand.

"It looks like a couple of you think you know. How about you in the back?" Mr. Hamlin pointed to Aki, who was sitting with the other percussionists.

"Rhythm," Aki spoke in his very deep voice.

"Close," Mr. Hamlin said encouragingly, "you're on the right track. How about you?" He was pointing to Cecilia.

She felt all the blood in her body rush to her face. She couldn't remember what had possessed her to put her hand in the air. She imagined she looked like a big talking red balloon, and right now, she just wanted to float away. She looked down at her book and then at Mr. Hamlin.

"Unison," she squeaked.

"That's what we're looking for," Mr. Hamlin praised.

Lou looked over and smiled at Cecilia. She thought she saw him raise his hand also but couldn't remember because she was so nervous about raising her own hand.

"What about this," Mr. Hamlin was standing in front of the piano once again. He used one hand to play three notes at once, but they sounded beautiful together.

Lou raised his hand before Cecilia could understand what Mr. Hamlin was trying to demonstrate, "That's a chord."

"Good job," Mr. Hamlin was ready to keep going until he noticed Thamyra Lirit step out of his office. "Who wants to volunteer next?" The same student who answered the last question was the next one to volunteer. "Go on in, and good luck."

Cecilia watched as Lou walked around her music stand and into the office. She remembered Mr. Hamlin saying something about waiting for execution. That is precisely what it felt like. Except this was more like waiting for a booster shot. Everyone has to do it even though it's slightly painful, but it's not like anyone would die from it.

"In a chord, several notes work together to create a special sound. What is this called?" Mr. Hamlin continued with class like it was any other day.

Cecilia's mind was swimming with all the vocabulary words she had crammed into her head for the written tests they had taken. She knew she had the answer, but it felt like her brain had just stopped working. Nothing happened when she tried to raise her hand or even open her mouth. She couldn't stop thinking about being all alone in that little room staring at the camera. What if her brain stopped working then too and she couldn't play at all? Even though Cecilia was convinced that her mind had stopped working, she was doing an awful lot of thinking. Suddenly her brain, her body, and her mouth all came to life at once- almost like she had been struck by lightning. Before she could catch up with herself, her hand was in the air.

"Ah, Cecilia. Do you know the word I'm looking for here?" Mr. Hamlin pointed right at her as he spoke.

Cecilia had almost forgotten that Mr. Hamlin had posed a question to the class, "No, sir. I want to volunteer to go next." She couldn't believe she had said it. Lorelei and Trilby both spun around and gazed at Cecilia quizzically.

"That's fine, dear, but do you know the answer? What is it called when we use chords to make music? What is it called when you play several notes at the same time and make a beautiful sound?" Mr. Hamlin could tell that everyone was having trouble staying on task with the playing test going on a room away. He would have to speed up to the good part if he wanted to keep their interest.

Once again, Cecilia's entire body broke down, but to her surprise, Lorelei had her hand high in the air, "Harmony."

Mr. Hamlin shifted his attention up one row to the student who had responded, "Excellent. When we get our instruments, the flutes will not play the same thing as the trumpets. Also, the tubas won't play the same thing as the clarinets. Right now, we all play the same notes and rhythms together, but we need to begin practicing a little harmony. Turn to page 26 in your practice books."

Lou came out and looked around the room trying to reassure the class that the test was not in any way painful. He wormed his way back to his chair, and as he sat down, Cecilia stood up. He looked up at her in silent shock. For a moment, she wanted to explain, but she couldn't start that kind of conversation in front of the whole class. She knew that she had to get it over with. She would never be able to concentrate on class while she was staring at the door, imagining the absolute worst.

She took her book and her recorder and walked toward Mr. Hamlin's office. She considered looking back and searching the room for a familiar and encouraging smile but reconsidered as she slowly closed the door behind her. When she turned around, she was face to face with the camera. The red light was on, and it was recording her every move.

She looked around before she sat in the chair in front of the camera. It was a small office, but it didn't feel small because there were large windows that displayed a panoramic view of the entire band room. Mr. Hamlin's desk was on the left side of the room. She almost didn't spot it because of all the sheet music covering its surface. An old clarinet was hanging on the wall next to a plaque with a silver baton attached to it. She couldn't read the plaque from the door, but she assumed it had been awarded to Mr. Hamlin because he was a good conductor and teacher. Her attention was quickly drawn back to the camera. She knew she had to get back on task.

She located the clipboard and took her time writing her name as neatly as possible, even though Lou had scribbled his name on the line above hers. She turned and looked at the camera. She said her name and began playing the scale she had memorized. She got two notes into it before she realized she hadn't told the camera what she would be playing. She stopped halfway through the scale and looked at the camera, "Oh, uh, I forgot to say the scale. E flat scale and arpeggio."

She wasn't stalling, although starting over from the beginning did help her relax. Nobody else was in the room. Nobody in the classroom could hear her. She took a deep breath and played the scale again without forgetting a single note. She made sure to play the arpeggio before she put her horn down to pick up her practice book.

"I'm going to play the song on page 21," her voice quivered as she spoke, but at least her hands weren't shaking. She was still nervous, but the test was halfway over now.

She tapped her foot to set the tempo and followed the notes to the song she had been perfecting all weekend. She pretended that she was the only person in the world, that way, if she messed up, she wouldn't get made fun of or laughed at. She stared at the practice book, making sure not to look up at the camera. Before she had time to try to calm down, it was over. She exhaled as she took her horn away from her lips. She looked up at the camera and then back down at her practice book. That was it. She didn't feel relieved until she stepped out of the room. She couldn't remember any other time when she was happy to be in front of a room full of people. She noticed they were about to play and quickly returned to her seat as another student got up and headed for Mr. Hamlin's office.

She plopped down next to Lou and put her horn to her lips even though she had no idea what they were about to play. The page Lou had opened in his practice book had a single title at the top, but there were three songs on the page. They were labeled A, B, and C. Lou pointed to the portion marked B and made eye contact with Cecilia. She took this to mean that this was what she should play and gave the line a quick scan to make sure she knew the fingerings for all the notes.

Cecilia didn't notice Mr. Hamlin had his hands in the air until she looked up at him. She felt guilty because she knew the whole class was waiting for her. He set the tempo and lowered his hands. Cecilia played the line Lou had pointed to, but the band sounded different this time. Everyone wasn't playing the same thing. The song was beautiful. Some students played notes with a very high pitch, and some played with a very low pitch. But everyone sounded wonderful together. Cecilia could tell that Lou was playing a different line of music than she was, but it sounded right. The playing test was no longer on her mind, and she could fully appreciate what was happening.

Once the song was over, Mr. Hamlin lowered his arms. The room was completely silent. Everyone looked around at one another in total amazement. None of them had any idea that they were capable of making that sound.

"Wonderful!" Mr. Hamlin wanted to jump up and down, "See how the notes work together to enhance the overall sound of the song. Let's try switching parts and playing that again."

Class continued quickly. Cecilia felt like everything was happening so fast that she couldn't keep up with the class or her thoughts. Volunteers were in and out of the office, but just as class was wrapping up, the brave volunteers stopped raising their hands, and it was time to go in alphabetical order.

"We're nearing the end of our hour. I'll check the tape of those of you who have already played. The rest of you will be called one at a time after warm-up tomorrow."

Instead of interrupting Mr. Hamlin today, the bell rang right after he was finished giving instructions. "Good job today, and good luck to those who have to test tomorrow," he managed to say over the crowd of students as they poured out of their chairs and into the busy hallway.

Trilby and Lorelei ran right over to Lou and Cecilia to ask them about the playing test. Cecilia looked knowingly at Lou but didn't say anything to him.

"What happens? Were you nervous? What did you play?" Lorelei was talking as loud as usual, but she was also talking very fast this time.

"Well, you practice at home, right?" Lou asked mockingly.

"Of course. How else do you memorize a scale?" Trilby

wanted real answers, and Lou's sarcasm was not in the least bit amusing to her.

"It's just like that, except a red light is staring at you." Lou looked at Cecilia for approval, but she was gathering her books and getting ready to leave.

"It's just like Lou says. And hey, at least you can practice some more tonight if you want," Cecilia didn't have anything else to say about the test. She was just happy it was over. "Caroline will go to home economics without me if I don't meet her in the hall," she quickly made her way out of the room.

The foot traffic was relatively swift, and Cecilia met up with Caroline as she came out of the chorus room, saying, "Hey, usually I'm waiting for you! How'd you get out so early?"

Cecilia laughed and replied, "I escaped certain death and great peril. Let's go."

Caroline joined her and asked, "Are you going to tell me about the test, or is that a sensitive issue?"

"Why would it be sensitive? I took it. No biggie." She tried to play it cool, but she was still recovering from the experience. "You know- we got to play some pretty cool stuff in class, too."

Caroline rolled her eyes and said, "At least you aren't playing Christmas music already! We rehearse for the Winter Concert every day, and it's not even Thanksgiving. You had regular class, and everyone took a playing test. How does that work?"

The previous class period flashed through her head in fast-forward, and she retold Caroline as much as possible without revealing how nervous she was. As she concluded her story, she realized she talked more about the time she spent in class than the actual test. She liked how Mr. Hamlin let them experiment with music. Today was a memorable day. They were one step closer to understanding the music like real musicians.

Just as they got within a few steps of the home economics classroom door, they heard a rude voice behind them, "Was that you swinging a bag of angry cats in the band room earlier."

Before either girl could respond, Moe said, "Dear brother, that was merely the wretched sound that comes from that weird flute Cecilia plays."

Cecilia knew they couldn't hear, but the thought of other students standing in the hall listening to her and laughing made her uneasy. She looked toward the classroom and then back at the Ditham brothers, "You two are going to make us late. Come on, Caroline."

This time Caroline stood her ground and glared back at Ben and Moe with her eyes squinted in anger, "Why don't you two find a cozy little corner somewhere and eat each other's boogers!" Cecilia had never seen her so angry, and she couldn't figure out what had set her off. She wanted to grab Caroline's arm and guide her closer to the door, but the teacher beat her to it.

"I'm sure you boys have a better place to be right now, don't you?" Mrs. Shannon asked Moe and Ben, "You two are going to make my students, as well as yourselves, late for class."

Cecilia knew the Ditham boys didn't care if they were late for class, but she was still glad Mrs. Shannon came along and steered everyone in the right direction. Both girls were led to class by the arm and allowed free once inside. They found a place together in the back row and sat in silence as class started.

Cecilia tore a piece of notebook paper and scribbled, *What was that about?* and placed it in front of Caroline. Mrs. Shannon did not stand for talking during class, but Cecilia and Caroline were slick about passing notes silently back and forth.

I'm tired of those two big mouth buttheads, Caroline candidly replied.

Me too, but you kinda freaked out back there! Cecilia responded and took a quick look at the front of the room to make sure Mrs. Shannon wasn't looking, but she was. She held the note in the palm of her hand and pretended that she had been paying attention. The only chance she had to pass the note was when Mrs. Shannon passed out a worksheet, but Caroline didn't have the opportunity to reply before class ended.

The bell rang, and Cecilia looked at Caroline blankly, hoping for a response to her earlier comment, but Mrs. Shannon appeared in front of them and blocked their path.

"I appreciate your discretion, ladies, but passing notes is just as distracting as carrying on a conversation." Caroline looked at Cecilia in shock as Mrs. Shannon continued to scold them, "I know this is the last class of the day, and it's hard to sit and listen to something that may not interest you. As a compromise, I will ignore your little written communication today. If this continues, I'll have to seat you two apart from now on. I don't want to do that. That's a tactic for elementary students, not middle school students who can sit still and hold their conversations until after class." The girls nodded in response as their teacher passed between them to get back to her desk.

"I didn't know she was watching," Cecilia said as soon as they stepped into the hallway.

"I didn't at first, but I thought she might be on to us. That's why I never wrote back," Caroline looked embarrassed even though it was over and they didn't get in any real trouble.

"So why did you lash out like that at Moe and Ben? I mean, they annoy me sometimes, but they've always been like that," Cecilia walked closely to Caroline, so she didn't lose her in the crowd of students headed out of the school.

"Look, it's like what you said that time about how you are going to be good at something, and they will only have each other and their bad habits to keep them happy," Caroline was trying to explain all this when Cecilia interrupted her.

"I believe what I said was that *we* would be good at something," she couldn't help correcting her.

"Okay, so *we* work hard to be good at something, and they stand in the hall and wait to make fun of us as we walk by,"

Caroline pointed out.

"They probably do it to everybody. We'll just try to ignore them from now on."

"That's not the point, Cecilia. They focus on people who can accomplish things and try to tear them down to a level that matches their lowly existence. I just don't like being part of their immature little name-calling game." Caroline wasn't as mad as she had been earlier, but Cecilia could tell she was still emotional about the whole thing.

"But they were making fun of me, not you," Cecilia pointed out.

"It doesn't matter. They shouldn't be making fun of anyone. Least of all, someone who worked as hard as you have to get where you are in band class," Caroline replied.

"Oh, please. I just took my first playing test. We've hardly done anything at all," Cecilia said modestly.

"How often did you get together with Trilby, Lorelei, and Lou to practice? How much did your brother help you study for those written tests? I've known you for a long time, and I've never seen you dedicate yourself to anything like you have with band class." Caroline stopped walking and looked right at Cecilia, "I don't want anyone to take that away from you."

Cecilia nodded in response, and the two walked quickly out to the front of the school. She was a little embarrassed that it took a spat with the Ditham brothers and Caroline's reaction to make her realize how hard she had worked. She had come a long way since the first day of school. It didn't feel like that much time had passed or that she had worked exceedingly hard to get there. But the fact was that months had passed, and she had memorized vocabulary, notes, and scales. She was days away from picking up her trumpet instead of her recorder. She smiled to herself as she waited patiently for Arion to arrive.

***

The next day was probably the easiest day Cecilia had ever had. It was completely different from the day before. Now she was filled with confidence and a comfort that made every aspect of the day slip by without tension or stress. Her friends, on the other hand, were nervous wrecks. This still did not affect her mood. She tried her best to put Lorelei and Trilby's minds at ease, but it didn't seem to work. She thought about how she felt the day before and how there wasn't much that someone could have said to her to make her relax (unless it was Mr. Hamlin telling her she didn't have to take the test, but that didn't happen).

Cecilia led the way to band class that day because Lorelei and Trilby seemed to be moving in slow motion. She was very glad she decided to take the test the day before. She proudly produced her recorder from her book bag and took her usual seat next to Lou. Looking around the room, she noticed the scene was like that of the day before. Everyone was huddled together, preparing for the playing test. Lou wasn't playing, but he wasn't observing the rest of the class like she was. He was talking to Thamyra Lirit. Lou usually got along with everyone, but Cecilia had never seen him speak to Thamyra before. Her curiosity got the best of her, and she leaned in for a listen.

"I knew it wouldn't be a big deal," Thamyra was commenting about the test that she was the first to take.

"It *is* a big deal. It just wasn't difficult," Lou replied, "The rest of the class isn't as experienced as you. Some of them had never seen written music until they stepped into this room."

"Good point," Thamyra agreed.

Cecilia got bored and slipped into the seat next to Lorelei, "Want to go over some scales together?"

Lorelei was one of the few members of her section who hadn't taken the test yet, so not many people around her were playing and preparing. "Please, just this scale to make sure I've got it down."

They played together until Mr. Hamlin came in. The bell had yet to ring, but Cecilia returned to her seat. Lorelei turned in her chair and mouthed a grateful "Thank you" to Cecilia just as Lou was settling in his seat.

"What was that about?" Cecilia asked Lou in a whisper, hoping Thamyra wasn't listening.

"Uh, well. She's been playing for a while. Her parents are both musicians. She is smug sometimes, but she is also very smart." Lou defended himself and Thamyra. He knew it was better to make friends than to establish enemies within the soon-to-be trumpet section.

"Excuse me. I didn't know you two were so close. Wanna switch seats so you can pass notes during class?" Cecilia asked sarcastically.

"We're not close. I'm just making nice. We will be in this class with these people all during the school year and probably next year too. I just don't want any bad blood between me and my classmates," Lou replied.

Cecilia knew he was right and smiled at him in agreement. She turned and managed a smile for Thamyra also. She wanted to say something, but the bell rang, and Mr. Hamlin started talking immediately.

"I've seen the tape from yesterday, and I am very impressed so far. I hope everyone who needs to play is here today. We will warm-up together, and when we finish, I will begin calling the rest of you in alphabetical order by last name. Ready? Hands up, horns up. Let's go!" He was charged and ready for class. Cecilia could feel the energy emitting off of him as he directed them through a few scales and the new song they learned the day before. He kept closing his eyes and letting his hands guide them through each note. It was like he enjoyed the feel of the music as much as the sound.

Cecilia followed along with the rest of the class but couldn't help noticing the people coming in and out of the office to take the playing test. It was amazing how stiff and tense everyone was as they walked into the office and how relaxed and accomplished they looked when they walked back out. It was weird watching everyone do what she had already done the day before. She knew what was happening in that room, and all she could do was hope that everyone was as prepared as she had been. She couldn't wait to hear Mr. Hamlin tell them to throw away their dumb ol' recorders and bring in real brass, wind, and percussion instruments.

Cecilia noticed that they had been playing the same thing over and over. Mr. Hamlin would isolate some sections to clear up any jumbled rhythms that weren't coming out within the harmony of the entire band. But when he brought the whole class in again, it was like they were playing a different song. They sounded like a band.

"This is wonderful! We've still got a few minutes left, but it seems that everyone has taken the test," Mr. Hamlin was as relieved as they were to have the playing test out of the way. "I still have to view the tape and give everyone a grade on their performance. This means we will still play our recorders for the rest of the week." A slight groan came from somewhere in the room. "I know you are all excited about playing your instruments, but we all have to go along at the same pace."

The bell rang, and it was all over. Lorelei smiled at Trilby, who smiled at Lou, who smiled at Cecilia. They had done it. They were one step closer to playing real instruments like a real band. Now they just had to wait.

Nobody was practicing their recorder after school anymore because soon, they wouldn't be playing them at all. Each day crept by slower than molasses on a cold day in winter. During band class everyone wanted to hear Mr. Hamlin say, "Make sure to bring your horns to class next time." It was the only thing anyone could think about. Although it seemed as though Mr. Hamlin had utterly forgotten about the test, the new horns, everything.

The last day of the week was as normal as any other. They were still playing recorders and pining away for the one announcement that would bring them all out of the spell of disappointment they were under. Cecilia had not forgotten how badly she wanted to play her trumpet, but she kept thinking it would never really happen. Her optimism had dwindled, and she strolled through the day as if she were convinced she would be bound to her silly little recorder forever. Band class began as usual, which further fueled Cecilia's doubt and filled her with a sadness she was not expecting. Everything had gone so well for so long that she never thought she would feel like this, but it did not last long.

Everyone was playing along, following the beat and accepting the fate of playing a toy for longer than they had expected. Suddenly Mr. Hamlin lowered his hands and put his baton down on his podium. The weight that had dragged everyone down for so long was about to be lifted. Cecilia felt butterflies in her stomach and could hardly sit still. Mr. Hamlin hadn't even spoken yet, but everyone could already feel the effect of his words.

"I have finished grading your playing test," Mr. Hamlin began with a simple statement. Every face in the room changed into an expectant smile that always reminded him why he enjoyed teaching so much. "I'll call each of you up to pick up an index card with your name and the numerical score for your playing test. That number is what I recorded in the grade book as your first playing test grade." It didn't take long for everyone to receive their score since they seemed to appear in front of Mr. Hamlin before he could finish reading the student's name. After the last student was seated, he continued, "If you have questions about your grade, please come see me after class. Speaking of your grade, I am prepared to offer extra credit to students who attend the Winter Concert. The chorus will be performing as well as the advanced 8th grade band. I'll add

10 points to your playing test score- that's a whole letter grade. For some of you, that will mean a potential score of 110."

Cecilia looked at Lou, and they both put their grade card on the music stand in front of them. They both had made the same score, 95. He looked up at her, and they silently shared their excitement and turned their attention back to the front of the room.

"I am very proud of how hard you have all worked, and I am thrilled to say that we are ready to put our recorders aside and bring our horns to class on Monday," He had to stop talking because the entire class had broken out in applause. He was glad to see everyone's enthusiasm even though they had no idea the hard work ahead of them.

"It's first come, first serve when it comes to cubby holes and shelf space," he paused to let everyone settle down and got their attention once again. "Let's use common sense, people. Please don't put your flute case in a hole big enough for a trumpet. You are welcome to use the larger spaces if you are willing to share. You are also welcome to drop your horn off on your way to first period if you have time. This will keep you from having to drag it around all day." He made this offer every year, but the first day the class brings their instruments to school, they always want to carry their horns so they can be seen with them. "When you come to class, sit where you normally do before you get your horns out. There will be some students from the high school here to help us get started, and I want you to assemble your horns under their instruction." He paused for effect and gave the room a once over, "We have worked hard to get this far, and we will have to work even harder to prepare for the concert at the end of the year. Enjoy your weekend, and remember to bring your horns, not your recorders, to class on Monday."

The bell hadn't rung, but Mr. Hamlin was finished, so he stepped down off the podium and made himself available for questions. Cecilia remembered when the Ditham boys tried in vain to break her recorder in half, and she suddenly wished it was possible to break it over her own knee. She looked up at Trilby and could tell by her expression that she had done well on the playing test. When she looked for Lorelei, she noticed that she had approached Mr. Hamlin holding her grade card. Cecilia elbowed Lou to get his attention and pointed toward Lorelei. He shrugged and continued the conversation he was having with the tuba player that sat behind him. She tried to get Trilby's attention to see what she thought, but she was too busy celebrating within her section and wasn't facing Cecilia's direction. The bell rang before Lorelei could return to her seat. Cecilia grabbed her things and made her way to the front of the room where Lorelei stood alone.

"What was that about?" Cecilia couldn't keep herself from asking.

"Nothing, I just thought I did better than this, is all. You know Trilby got a perfect score." Lorelei's voice was no longer loud and proud but flat and somber.

"Hey, there's the extra credit thing. I'll probably go." Cecilia tried to sound upbeat. It was a time to celebrate, and she couldn't be happy when her friend was so sad.

"Yeah, I can do that, but what about when we get our real horns? How am I supposed to play a saxophone if I can't play this dumb thing? I got it, you know. It has way more buttons on it than this," she waved the recorder in the air recklessly as she spoke. Cecilia suddenly understood Lorelei's problem, but she had no time to sympathize.

"Hey, let's go, or I'm leaving without you," Caroline was standing inside the band room calling for Cecilia.

"Just go. You'll be late. It's over. We did it. I'll just focus on that," Lorelei tried to sound cheerful, but Cecilia didn't buy it. She gave her a playful nudge and ran to catch Caroline who had already made her way into the hall.

She appeared at Caroline's side and said, "You've got to get moving, or you're going to make me late," she scolded mockingly. Caroline rolled her eyes in response and began walking faster.

As they got closer to class, Cecilia noticed the Ditham boys weren't in the hall, "Hey, where are Beavis and Butthead today?"

"Who cares," Caroline commented.

"I was going to give them my recorder since they seem to like it so much," Cecilia said casually.

Caroline stopped walking, but Cecilia continued on as if what she said meant nothing. "Wait," Caroline pulled on Cecilia's book bag to slow her down. "What are you saying? I mean, I heard you. But…what?"

Cecilia could tell she was excited for her, and she hadn't even heard the words yet, "They seemed to like it so much, and it doesn't look like I'll need it anymore."

Caroline hugged her so hard that she almost lifted her feet off the ground, "This is it, you know. It all starts here."

Cecilia nodded. She did know. After all the anticipation, she still couldn't believe it was happening. The bell rang.

"Oh, no." Caroline and Cecilia sprinted the few steps left to the classroom doorway, but both of them were still met with a disapproving glare from Mrs. Shannon.

Chapter Eight

The weekend floated by. Cecilia slept late and watched cartoons all day, just like she did every weekend. Only this time, she looked at the TV, but she wasn't paying attention to what was happening. She kept imagining what class would be like on Monday. She was also trying to distract herself from her excitement. She wanted to pretend like everything was normal until she brought her horn down with her Monday morning. She sat quietly and snacked on cereal right out of the box as if her life had not changed.

Her plan worked. Not one member of the family was suspicious. Why would they be? She had practically held her breath for the last two days waiting for this moment. She woke up before her alarm went off and silently got dressed, eyeballing the trumpet case the whole time. She waited until she heard her mother in the kitchen making breakfast before she came out of her room. She put her book bag strap over her shoulder and gripped the handle of her trumpet case with the other hand. It was weightless. It was hovering next to her as if it had a motor and wings. It pulled her out of the room and guided her to the stairs. She couldn't remember moving her feet to get down the hall. It felt like the magic of the case had taken hold of her and was making her levitate instead of walk.

She came to the bottom of the stairs and heard her mother's voice, "Your sister had better hurry. I'm not writing notes if you're late."

"It's okay. I'm ready," She stood in the doorway so her mother and brother could get a good look at her.

"Wait! Something's different," Arion tried to be sarcastic, but nothing could ruin this for Cecilia.

"Have you been keeping this a secret all weekend? We'll have to celebrate tonight, then." Her mother kissed her forehead and gave her a big hug. "I just wish your father hadn't left for work already. He'd want to see this."

"See what?" Cecilia still tried to act casual.

"Come on, squirt. Do you think I can't read the signs? That's obviously *not* a recorder in your hand." Arion sounded genuinely excited for her.

"Trumpet or not, you've got to get to school." Leave it to mom to bring everyone back to reality, "I'll make your favorite supper tonight, okay."

Cecilia continued to float as she left the house and got in the car. She was too excited to talk. She held her trumpet case handle the whole ride to school. She kept looking in the floorboard to make sure it was still there.

"It's not going to disappear," Arion joked as he noticed Cecilia's obsession with the trumpet case at her feet.

"I know that. It's just a relief carrying this instead of a piece of plastic," she looked down at the case again.

"Well, good luck," Arion said as Cecilia gathered her backpack and trumpet case.

She stepped out of the car and looked at the front doors of the school. The intimidating building that towered over her on the first day seemed to shrink slowly at the mere sight of the trumpet case in her hand. The sensation that she was floating intensified when she entered the building. All eyes shifted around the hallway, but they each stopped in Cecilia's direction. They knew. The whole school knew.

Cecilia saw several of her band classmates in the hall on her way to homeroom. They were also proudly carrying their instrument cases. She shared a secret smile with each of them as they crossed her path. It's as if they were all in the same exclusive club- a band geek club.

When she reached Mrs. Tallbay's classroom, she noticed that Lorelei had already taken her seat. She was using her saxophone case to reserve the seat next to her for Cecilia. "Right here," Lorelei said and waved.

Cecilia put her trumpet case next to her desk and her backpack on the back of her chair, "Hey, ready for band?"

Lorelei patted her saxophone case, "Oh yes, we're ready."

"I never heard how you did on the playing test last week," Cecilia casually observed, hoping that Lorelei would tell her why she had to talk to Mr. Hamlin after class.

"I did okay," her expression and her voice exposed her true emotions, and Cecilia was not fooled.

"Come on. It can't be that bad. Everyone must have passed because today we get to play these," she motioned to the instrument cases that lay between them.

"Let's just say I'm going to the Winter Concert this Friday," Lorelei was hinting at how necessary it was for her to get the extra credit points.

Cecilia could hear the disappointment in her voice and wanted to do something to make her feel better. "Hey," the idea came out of her mouth at the same time it entered her brain, "Let's all go! We can make it a thing. We can have the 7th grade band student section. It'll be fun. This way, we can see what performing in concert is like."

Lorelei looked at her with renewed hope and optimism, "You think we could do that? It would be so fun if we all could go." She was so grateful that Cecilia had made the suggestion. That way, all her friends could go, and she didn't have to admit that she made a C on her playing test.

Cecilia continued to reassure her insecure friend, "Oh yeah, we can tell Trilby and Lou later and ask our parents tonight."

By the time the bell rang for first period, Lorelei's mood had improved considerably, and Cecilia felt better for having something to do with it. They each grabbed their horn cases and headed for class. "See you in english," Cecilia said as she stepped into Mr. Duke's classroom.

The day progressed like any other. Cecilia was so excited that time didn't seem to exist anymore. Social studies was more tedious than usual, and there was a substitute teacher for Mrs. Bilge, so math class consisted of word problem worksheets and other busy work. None of it seemed to faze Cecilia or alter her high spirits. She just coasted through the day, and everything that happened rolled off her back like rainwater. The whole morning seemed like a dream that could neither harm nor change her.

Once Cecilia reached English class and could consult with Lorelei and Trilby about band class, the excitement slowly began to build. The three of them sounded like a gaggle of geese at a cocktail party. They each spoke on top of the next, but somehow, they all knew what was being said. Class ended in a flash, and on the way to the band room, all three girls seemed to experience the same floating feeling Cecilia had felt all day.

The anticipation was contagious, and the whole school seemed to feel it. It was like a ghost was floating aimlessly through the halls, the other students knew something was different, but no one could put their finger on the cause.

The closer they got to exploratory hall, the more band students they came across. Everyone had the same confident expression on their face. There was a line to get into the band room because everyone was trying to get situated in the correct section and seat. After entering, she noticed several unfamiliar faces and automatically assumed they were the high school students brought over to help. She separated from Lorelei and Trilby without a word and went to her usual seat next to Lou.

No one had their instrument out yet, but some people were holding their cases in their laps, hoping they would get to open them soon. The room was filled with nervous excitement that even seemed to affect Mr. Hamlin. He was beaming with pride and brimming with suspense, and it was written all over his face. Before the bell could ring, he was already giving instructions.

"I know we are all excited today, but we have a lot to get through before we play. You will play today. First things first, we will have to scatter a bit so that each section can get started on its own. These talented young people from the Brementon High School marching band have taken time out of their busy schedules to help us today. Listen to them as if they were me talking to you. We will get the entire band together to try a scale or two before class ends." Mr. Hamlin spoke plain and clear even though the thoughts in his head were going a mile a minute. He made his way to each section to introduce the students to their instructor and direct them to a corner of the room to practice. He sent the percussion section out into the music hall so they could have a little more privacy and didn't distract the rest of the band.

Cecilia sat straight up as Mr. Hamlin came towards the trumpet section. She looked at Lou, and they shared a big smile.

"Trumpet section, this is Nina Kulitta," Mr. Hamlin gestured toward the girl standing next to him. "She will lead you to the back left section of the room and hand out your practice books." He nodded at the group of them and moved to the saxophone section.

The entire section was fixated on the girl standing in front of them. Nina wasn't intimidating at all. She was of average height with a kind face and long dark hair. She held a trumpet casually in her left hand and the mouthpiece in her right. She herded the seven members of the trumpet section to the back of the room where Mr. Hamlin had earlier indicated. She was a little nervous. This was her first workshop, and she felt underqualified for the task. She had never even done an instrument demonstration before, but Mr. Alvis specifically requested that she participate in this workshop. As she handed out the practice books, she finally decided to speak to the group.

"Here are your practice books," She would have also said the word "duh" if it weren't so old school. She took a slow, deep breath and tried again, "Let's start by getting our horns out." She was starting to loosen up a bit, "There are only two pieces that you have to assemble, the mouthpiece and the horn." She held up the items in her hands so the entire section could get a good view. "The mouthpiece fits right in here with a gentle twist," She was still holding her horn in the air as she spoke, "Be careful. It's not a jar of pickles. If you use too much force, the mouthpiece can get stuck." She gave each of them a moment to experiment with their horns and observed carefully to make sure each one was doing it correctly.

Cecilia immediately learned what Nina meant when she said to be gentle. The first time she assembled her trumpet, the mouthpiece got stuck. She looked to her right, where Thamyra Lirit was expertly inserting and removing her mouthpiece with ease. Cecilia was too embarrassed to ask her for help, so she turned to her left, where Lou was assembling his trumpet properly. She swallowed her pride and asked, "Could you give me a pull?" She held her horn up so Lou could get a grip, and the mouthpiece popped right off. She gave it another try and was successful in assembling and disassembling her trumpet. She smiled to herself and looked up to share her expression with Nina.

Nina applauded Cecilia with an encouraging smile and laid her horn in the chair closest to her. "Now that you've put them together take the mouthpiece out of the horn and put the horn down under your lap."

Cecilia did what she was told but thought it was an odd request. How can they learn to play if they aren't holding their horns? She looked around the room to see if anyone else was doing anything weird like they were. She was utterly surprised at what she saw. Not only were other sections doing what they were, but some looked even weirder. Lorelei and the rest of the saxophone and clarinet sections were sucking on what looked like wooden popsicle sticks. Trilby and the flutes were blowing through their mouthpieces, but they hadn't assembled their horns entirely yet. Cecilia felt better about what she was doing and followed Nina's instructions, no matter how odd it seemed.

"This is all you need to make sound," Nina put the mouthpiece to her lips and made a low buzzing sound with it. "The trumpet takes that little noise and pipes it through the valves, so the finished product is a beautiful brassy sound." She put the mouthpiece on the horn and played a note to demonstrate her point. When she finished, she put the horn right back where it was in the chair next to her. "There is one other important part of the instrument that can affect the sound." It wasn't a question, but it got the group of them thinking.

Cecilia looked down at her horn and tried to think of what Nina was talking about. She glanced at Lou, who was also looking quizzically at his own horn. She turned to Thamyra Lirit, who sat and stared at Nina, hoping she could somehow read the answer off her face.

"I'll give you a hint," Nina offered after she noted the section's response, "It doesn't fit in your horn case."

Now they were really confused. Thamyra furrowed her brow in frustration. Cecilia exhaled loudly in an exasperated breath of defeat. Her aggravation at the situation left her body with that breath of air. She cleared her mind and prepared to take another cleansing breath when it suddenly came to her.

Just as Nina had given up on one of them answering her, Cecilia spoke, "Air."

The word felt like it slapped Nina in the face. She looked at Cecilia and realized that she was faced with genuine excitement and curiosity for music. Each one of these students was bursting with expectations.

"Yes," Nina said, "That's exactly it. You make the air that buzzes in the mouthpiece and goes through the trumpet. The air needs a clear path to the horn to make the right sound." Again, she assembled her trumpet to make her point. She stood tall with her shoulders square and played a long, beautiful note. Then she slouched, stood with her shoulders slumped, and played the same note. The difference was clear to the amateur ears of the students listening. The second time she played, the note was distorted and not near as pleasant as the sound she had previously made.

"Posture is what makes or breaks your overall sound," Nina sat in the chair she put her trumpet in earlier, "Sit on the front half of the seat with your legs like this and your shoulders and arms like this." She sat up straight and tall in the chair but kept her eye on the students as they experimented with what she was showing them. "Good," she thought it was time to make an encouraging remark. She wasn't used to teaching and didn't know what to do with herself. She knew she was doing the right thing as long as she had their attention. "Picture yourself as a flagpole, and your trumpet is the flag. The only difference here is that you must picture that the wind is always blowing. Keep the horn straight out in front of you. If the bell of your horn begins to fall below the music stand, you need to adjust your posture." She slowly slunk down in the chair and aimed her trumpet at the floor to show them how easy it was to forget to hold the position.

The whole section sat up with their hands in front of them, holding an invisible trumpet. Cecilia felt absolutely ridiculous until she glanced around the room and noticed that most of the other sections were doing the same thing. No one had even played a real note yet.

"All right," Nina stood and faced the section, "Buzz your lips like you're making a bee noise." She demonstrated it so they would copy exactly what she was doing.

Cecilia thought Thamyra Lirit sounded the loudest, certainly louder than Lou. The entire section made the most absurd faces while making this weird buzzing noise. It would have been embarrassing if they hadn't all been doing it together under the instruction of an actual trumpet player.

Nina looked at their faces and remembered what it was like when she first learned how to play. She was frustrated, but she wanted to play so badly that she was determined enough to suffer through the beginning to get where she is now. She was getting the hang of teaching the small group and was eager to take the lesson to the next level.

"Let's make that same noise into our mouthpiece. Put your lips tightly together and begin making the noise just after you put the mouthpiece to your lips," She instructed and then listened. She noticed some students having trouble buzzing with the mouthpiece in front of them, so she tended to them one at a time until everyone was making the same buzzing sound.

Cecilia noticed Thamyra Lirit had no problem making sounds with her mouthpiece, but she had played before. She might even know a scale or two. Suddenly Cecilia became very self-conscious about sitting next to someone so much more experienced than her. She listened carefully and tried in vain to make the same sound as Nina and Thamyra. Lou fumbled with the buzzing at first but quickly mastered the skill. Cecilia caught herself slouching in defeat and promptly sat upright, took another deep breath, and exhaled into her mouthpiece. Still not quite right. She was the only one in the section who couldn't do it.

Nina appeared at her side and offered more assistance, "Buzz for me." If anyone had made that request before, Cecilia probably would have laughed herself sick, but right now, she was under pressure and the word buzz transformed from silly to serious. Nina buzzed with her. She looked closely at how her lips worked to make the sound. Cecilia tried pursing her lips even more, making them as tight as she could and still have air come out of her mouth. When she put the mouthpiece to her lips and buzzed, Nina's face lit up. That was enough to encourage Cecilia to continue making the noise with confidence, along with the other members of her section.

After another minute of buzzing, Nina silenced the group with a confident wave of her hand. She picked up her horn and instructed the others to do the same. She demonstrated how to insert the mouthpiece one more time, but this time she left it in her horn. Cecilia could feel herself jittering with excitement, waiting to play her trumpet for the first time.

"Here's an easy question," Nina began again, "How many valves are on a trumpet?"

"Three," everyone answered in unison.

"Well, there may be only three valves, but there are many, many notes. By blowing into the horn, you use your lips to change the tone and the note you are playing," She stopped talking and held her horn to her lips. She didn't press any valves, but she played different notes. "When you begin playing a song or a scale, you must make sure you begin with the correct note. This is especially problematic when you practice alone, and you can't compare your sound to the rest of the section."

Suddenly the room was filled with the whispering whistle of the flute section. They were the first to play a note with their horns. The whole room stopped what they were doing and listened to the flutes. Mr. Hamlin quickly ran right over to congratulate them.

"We'll get there," Nina explained, "I just need to show you how to hold your horn properly, and then we can play our first note." She was ready to get to the good part. "With your right hand, you grip the top of the horn with your pinky in this little hook," she pointed to what she was talking about and then showed them how to put their fingers over the valves. "Halfway there, now with your left hand, simply grip the valve casings on the left side of the trumpet." She held her horn and walked by each of them to make sure they were following her lead. "Show me your posture and put your horn to your mouth, but do not play yet." Again, she passed by each of them, correcting them as she went, and she was sure they were ready to play.

Cecilia was concentrating on keeping very still. She wasn't used to sitting like this, and she was very uncomfortable. Thamyra Lirit was right at home, and Lou seemed to automatically adjust to any situation. She looked up and noticed Lorelei squirming in her chair, and it made her feel better to see someone who felt the same way she did. The flute section broke the silence once again when they slowly made their way through the notes of a scale. Cecilia reminded herself to sit up straight and looked at Nina for more instruction.

"When you played recorders, did you come across the B flat scale?" Nina knew they were playing scales and short songs, but she didn't want to assume anything.

"We had to memorize it for warm-up," Thamyra finally got the opportunity to speak. Cecilia could tell it was killing her to sit silently while the rest of them baby step their way through this whole process.

"Let's try to play the first note of that scale. You don't have to push any valves. You must use your ears to find the right note and adjust the sound with your lips. Don't forget about your posture and breathing." Nina rattled off everything they needed to know to play a note. Now it was time to play.

Cecilia went through a checklist in her head, so she didn't forget what Nina said. Just as they were about to break the silence with their victorious note, the saxophone section beat them to it. A squawk and a squeak here and there, but most of them were playing the right note.

Nina kept her horn up but turned to see the saxophones play. When she turned back to her section, she faced seven expectant students ready to play. She put the horn to her mouth and directed with her left hand. She raised her hand and lowered it, expecting an awful noise to hit her ears. One student, in particular, was definitely playing the right note, and it didn't take long for the rest of them to poke around and find the right one. She slowly cut them off, "Okay, now you know what the note sounds like. Let's try again." She cued them once again, and this time, she was met with the same confused chord, but the longer they played the note, the easier it was for them all to sound the same.

Mr. Hamlin ran over to applaud his trumpet section, "This is wonderful. Keep this up, and we might play a scale before the bell rings!"

Nina had never heard anyone so excited about playing a scale, but then she thought about the first time she played the B flat scale on her trumpet from memory. Suddenly her nostalgia recharged her, and she faced the group with more confidence than before.

"Open up the practice book I gave each of you earlier and let's find the B flat scale," said Nina. "Here, on page 3." She held the book up so they could all see. "Take a look at the notes and the fingering chart underneath."

The first thing Cecilia noticed was how easy it was to read the trumpet fingering chart. Since there were only three valves, the possibilities were limited and much less complicated than the recorder fingering chart she was studying the week before. She also remembered that Thamyra Lirit had bragged that she already knew this particular scale on her trumpet. Cecilia focused on the notes and how to finger each one correctly. Their horns were in the air again, ready to play the scale.

Nina held up her horn so the group could see which notes she was playing and play along with her. She cued them with her hand, and they slowly changed notes together. It suddenly hit her why Mr. Alvis had asked her to do this workshop. She forgot why she liked playing. She worked so hard to memorize her music and practice every day that it had become a chore. Looking at this room full of students excited to play a scale reminded her of the wonderful effects music can have on people, including herself.

It wasn't long before each section was playing the scale and mastering the basics of their instrument. Mr. Hamlin called everyone back to the center of the room just before class was about to end. The band assembled in their proper sections, and each student held a real instrument.

"Class went by so fast," Mr. Hamlin announced, "We only have time to try a scale. We'll add drums next time. Turn to page 3, and we can try the B flat scale together. Hands up, horns up. You know the drill by now."

Cecilia had barely gotten her posture right when Mr. Hamlin's hands were in the air. She put her horn to her lips. She quickly took a glance at the rest of the class. It was beautiful. Everyone sat proudly with their brass and woodwind instruments, ready to play. This was the moment she had been waiting for. Mr. Hamlin lowered his hands, and the entire band played together with real instruments. It was the most horrible din Cecilia had ever been in the same room with. He kept his hands up, not changing the note. Certain sections adjusted their posture and fingering, and suddenly everyone was playing the same note. Cecilia felt the whole room fill up with bass, brass, wind, and herself. Mr. Hamlin moved his hand, and the band changed notes together. This time it was even the right note. Up and up and back down the scale they had played so many times on their recorders. Now they were real musicians with real instruments.

Once they had finished the scale, the class noticed that they had an audience. The chorus had stuck their heads in for a listen. Caroline was right in front and started a round of applause in honor of the performance. Mr. Hamlin proudly bowed, gestured to the band, and said, "They did all the hard work. I just waved my arms in the air."

It was at this exact inopportune moment that the bell rang. The members of the chorus scattered to get their books and head to class. The band class was scrambling to get their horns put away so they could do the same.

"Make sure you take your horns home and practice tonight!" Mr. Hamlin reminded the class as they left the room.

By the time Cecilia got her horn back in its case, the whole class had left already, and Caroline was tapping her foot impatiently by the band room door. She decided to carry her horn instead of storing it in one of the cubbyholes. The whole class pretty much decided to do the same. Cecilia wondered if she would ever use one. She liked carrying her horn around.

Caroline began coaxing Cecilia before she reached the doorway, "Come on, we are on the verge of tardiness." They both picked up the pace, but Cecilia knew they weren't going to make it. The hall was practically empty, and those who remained were running. The bell rang just as they were two steps outside the home economics lab.

"Girls," Mrs. Shannon pronounced when Cecilia and Caroline entered the room, "This is your second tardy this semester." She watched as they worked their way quickly to their seats, "Ah, maybe your new dead weight held you back." She was, of course, referring to Cecilia's horn case.

Cecilia did not like the way Mrs. Shannon called her trumpet "dead weight," but she rattled off an excuse anyway, "It took too long to put my horn away after class. I didn't realize I was making both of us tardy." She tried her best to get Caroline off the hook.

"Well," Mrs. Shannon changed to a kinder tone of voice than she had used before, "Let's not make it a habit, ladies."

Cecilia looked at Caroline, and without a word, they both wondered whether she ever marked them tardy or not. They shrugged silently and made sure to behave in an attempt to avoid further scolding.

Since the holidays were fast approaching, Mrs. Shannon spent the class period discussing the operation of basic kitchen appliances in preparation for common holiday foods. Cecilia found the discussion about toaster ovens particularly interesting since she had always used a regular toaster. Caroline was bored out of her mind but didn't show it in her face or body language. She just focused on the direction of the teacher and zoned out.

By the time class was over, Cecilia had an overwhelming urge to prepare fresh bread and green bean casserole while following proper home economic safety guidelines. They managed to make it out of the room without another confrontation with Mrs. Shannon about their tardiness.

"So," Caroline was the first to speak, "you guys sounded great today!"

Cecilia couldn't help but laugh out loud, "You're too nice for your own good. It was a train wreck without the mess."

"You don't give yourself enough credit," Caroline was trying to sound encouraging. "You had to practice to get this far, so you'll practice some more and get better. Right?"

Cecilia nodded and held the door with her foot so Caroline could pass. "You know we might be going to that Christmas concert."

Caroline stopped for a second and looked at Cecilia before continuing, "Who is *we*?"

"You know," Cecilia walked faster, "All of us. We still have to ask, but we get extra credit in band if we go. So...."

Caroline quickly cut her off, "Who is *all of us*?"

Cecilia was thrown off by Caroline's seriousness: "Uh, me, Lorelei, Trilby, Lou. It's mainly for Lorelei. I don't think she did so well on her playing test. But you know...."

Caroline interrupted her again, "So you're all going to be there. Sitting together. I see."

Cecilia was completely mystified by Caroline's response. She thought she would be happy to see a few familiar faces in the crowd, but it seemed to make her nervous and agitated instead.

They got to the front of the school, and it was time for Cecilia to break away and board the bus, "I gotta go. You okay?"

Caroline smiled while she nodded and then turned to walk the other way. Cecilia wrinkled her forehead in absolute confusion. She couldn't figure out what would possess Caroline to react the way she had to the notion that they would all be at the concert. She boarded the bus and got a seat to herself because she put her trumpet case up next to her, blocking the space for anyone else to claim. She calmly rested her arm on top of her horn case and flicked the handle back and forth from time to time.

When she got home, the house was silent. Both of her parents were still at work, and Arion was at practice preparing for the last game of the playoffs. She immediately went to her room and got her horn out. Now was her chance to practice with nobody around. She put her practice book on the end of her desk and sat up as straight as she could. It was hard not to slouch in her comfy chair, but she tried to focus on the book and keep her horn up.

She got frustrated really fast. She couldn't pick out the right note to start on. When she finally found the note, she was slouching in defeat, and it didn't sound right. The fingerings were easy. She memorized those before she could figure out how to play the notes. She just couldn't figure out which note to start on. It was easier in class because she could listen and play what Lou or Thamyra were playing. But she was alone now and had no idea how to start. She'd try to start the scale, but by the third note, she realized she wasn't playing it correctly. Her lips began to ache. She put the horn back in its case and threw the practice book across the room in defeat.

She knew she wouldn't be perfect, but she had no idea she would be this bad. The rest of the week was as discouraging as the first day had been for Cecilia. Even with her friends and the rest of the band, she still couldn't get the hang of her sound. She couldn't just raise her horn and play a note. She would play a note and poke around until she sounded like everyone else. When Mr. Hamlin added the percussion section, it only added to Cecilia's frustration. She could feel the drumbeats all the way inside her stomach, making it difficult to find her place in the music.

At one point, she thought Lorelei might share her aggravation as she watched her shake her saxophone rather violently during class. It turned out she was shaking the rest of the spit off of the bottom of her horn. Cecilia watched the little blob of moisture drip to the floor and crashed into itself as it hit the little puddle Lorelei created beneath her.

When it was time to go to the Christmas concert, she wanted to back out and stay home, but Lorelei's face reminded her of the promise she had made to her friend. She slowly got in the front of the car and waited for everyone else to pile into the back and buckle up. Lou sat in the middle of the backseat with Trilby and Lorelei on each side.

Once they got underway, Lorelei asked, "Did you tell Caroline we were coming?"

Cecilia remained buckled but turned in her seat a bit to face her friends in the back, "Yeah, it was weird. She got all serious and kept asking who all was coming."

"Huh," Lou looked at Trilby and Lorelei, and they were equally unaware of why Caroline would respond the way she did. "Maybe she has to wear a goofy costume like we did for that pageant in third grade."

"Come on, we're not in elementary school anymore," Trilby blurted out.

"Well, her mother sure is proud," Cecilia's mother explained, "She went on and on about Caroline getting that solo part."

Cecilia spun around again, "That must be it. She didn't say anything to me about a solo. She might be nervous or something."

"Oh, we've heard Caroline sing before. What's so big about now?" Lorelei asked.

"It's a solo, as in all alone—in front of everybody," Cecilia explained.

"Firing squad," Lou said while gesturing his hands as if shooting a gun.

"It can't be that bad," Lorelei said as casually as she could but slowly realized what they meant.

"Do you want to stand up in front of all those parents and teachers and play your saxophone all alone?" Trilby asked Lorelei.

"Well, no." Lorelei looked at the back of Mrs. Banbury's seat and thought about how horrible it would, in fact, be.

"So, we support her and tell her she did well no matter what," Lou suggested.

"Look," Cecilia did not turn around this time, "She's talented, otherwise, she wouldn't have been chosen to sing a solo. She'll be fine."

The whole car mumbled in agreement as they parked next to the school. Cecilia and her friends unbuckled and jumped out of the car.

"Hold up, kids," Mrs. Banbury yelled after them. "Meet me at the car after the concert." They all nodded and waved, but she wanted a verbal response from her daughter to make sure she understood. "Cecilia, *right* after the concert!"

"Okay," Cecilia managed to holler before she ran inside the school.

The auditorium was beautifully decorated for the season. Holly was pinned at the end of each row of seats with red and green streamers as far as the eye could see. The tree was real and at least fifteen feet tall. Cecilia was in awe of both its size and beauty. Covered in bright white lights and giant silver ornaments, it commanded attention with its sheer brilliance.

"Let's sit near the tree," Cecilia suggested.

"Okay, but I want the aisle seat," Lorelei blurted before anyone else could claim it.

Trilby led the way, "This all right?"

Once they were seated, Lou began scanning the crowd for familiar faces, "Look, there's that tuba player and that really tall drummer."

"Hey," Trilby stood and waved at someone. "She's in my section," she explained as she sat back down.

Cecilia did see a few people she recognized from band class, "I don't see Thamyra Lirit."

"Like she needs extra credit," Lou replied.

"True," Cecilia agreed, "I just assumed this would be the kind of thing she would be drawn to."

A student usher approached their row and began passing out the program for the concert. Cecilia quickly flipped it open and looked for mention of a solo.

"The chorus performs first, and then the band plays," Trilby spoke but was still reading the program in her hands.

"Yeah, but look," Lou noted, "They play something together in the middle."

"'Greensleeves,'" Cecilia was talking to herself, but Lorelei responded.

"Hey, that's the solo. Her name is in here and everything," Lorelei pointed to show Trilby.

"Caroline Fenten; soloist," Lou read aloud.

Cecilia stared at the words until it felt like they were burned into her brain. She couldn't imagine her name in the same place. It wasn't that she didn't want it there. She wanted to be a great musician, but the notion of playing solo reminded her of how inexperienced she was with her horn. She could barely get through a scale all alone in her room. The house lights gave a quick blink. Cecilia put her program in her lap and gave her full attention to the stage.

The curtain opened, and the chorus was already standing there. They all wore black pants, a white shirt, and a Santa hat. Cecilia was surprised that they weren't forced to wear something more humiliating. She recognized every song on the program, but she was most anxious to hear Caroline's solo. She picked her out of the whole chorus even though she was in the next to last row. The audience applauded supportively to welcome the chorus to the stage.

The entire auditorium was immediately filled up with music. It was the most wonderful sound Cecilia had ever heard. She looked down the row at her friends, who seemed equally impressed with the performance. She expected the sound of carolers or a sing-along, but she was hearing real singers with expressive voices and cooperative harmony.

The Christmas music possessed Cecilia with the spirit of the season and the pride that comes from watching someone you care about succeed. She almost forgot she was seated in the school auditorium. She could have been in a church sanctuary or a grand music hall. She sang along in her head to the songs she knew by heart as she heard Lorelei loud and clear as she sang along out loud. Trilby was fully prepared to silence her but couldn't bring herself to do it. When she turned and saw the look on her friend's face, she smiled and nodded along to the music.

Suddenly there was an odd break in the program, and the chorus was quiet. Cecilia looked down the row at the rest of her friends, who seemed equally confused. The chorus stood in silence and looked out as if it were the audience's turn to perform.

Lou consulted his program and whispered, "It's time for the band to come out."

Trilby asked, "What about the solo?"

The stage curtains opened wider to reveal the empty seats where the band would sit. Mr. Hamlin was nowhere to be seen, but the band obediently filed onto the stage. Cecilia noticed that Caroline no longer stood in the back of the chorus. She was standing out front, center stage.

"This is it," Cecilia responded more eagerly than she intended. Lou pointed to the song "Greensleeves" in the program and held it out for Trilby and Lorelei to see.

Cecilia couldn't decide whether to focus on the band or on Caroline. She watched her stand motionless and expressionless in front of the chorus. Firing squad. Out of the corner of her eye, she saw Mr. Hamlin come out on the stage. The audience began clapping once again and caught Cecilia off guard. Mr. Hamlin gestured to the band, and they all took their seats simultaneously.

There was a brief second when both the directors looked at one another to synchronize the beat. When Mr. Hamlin turned, he counted off the beat, and the band started playing. Cecilia looked at the band and then back to the chorus. The entire chorus stood like statues and looked out at all the people looking right back at them.

Cecilia took a big breath in and, for a moment, felt as if she were inhaling the music. She could feel the notes bounce off her teeth and the drumbeats in her belly. Before she could exhale, it stopped. Mr. Hamlin cut the band off. Cecilia was about to turn to her friends again when she noticed the chorus director raise her arms. She knew from band class that the beautiful music would begin again when her hands came down.

She was right. The beautiful music did begin, but it wasn't the big chorus she had heard earlier. The only sound was Caroline's voice. It entranced the entire audience the way a siren puts her musical spell on unsuspecting sailors. It wasn't only the lyrical magic that sprang from Caroline's voice that impressed her friends. She was confident. She closed her eyes and let the music take her to a place where there was no audience, parents, or her friends glaring at her. She was in her own private bubble that gave her an unyielding boost of confidence.

With one quick whip of the directors' batons, the chorus and the band joined Caroline. She stepped back in line, and her voice melted in with all the others. Cecilia felt like she was watching a tennis match as she kept looking back and forth from the band to the chorus. The two groups together created such a full sound. So much was happening all at once, and Cecilia was utterly surprised at what she may someday be capable of. When the song ended, the audience exploded with applause. Some proud parents even stood and waved to their talented son or daughter. The chorus slowly filed out of the risers they were standing on and sat together on the left side of the auditorium.

"I wondered who those seats were reserved for," Lorelei noted softly.

Lou nodded and consulted his program, "Check it out," he pointed to the next song, "It's a percussion solo."

Cecilia leaned in before remembering she had a program of her own. She read the word xylophone and looked up toward the stage at a row of them right in front. They began playing "Carol of the Bells," which was another song Cecilia knew. She almost forgot that a xylophone was a percussion instrument. She was surprised to hear drummers playing without the band. But she also noticed that they seemed to be having a lot of fun.

They played the whole song without the band. As soon as they finished, the band began playing the next song in the program. The drummers rolled the xylophones to the back of the stage and quickly joined the rest of their section.

Cecilia was as mesmerized with the band as she had been with the chorus. Each song was familiar, but there was always a surprise. A saxophone player jazzed up the ending to "Rudolf the Red-Nose Reindeer," and the trumpet section stole the show during "Jingle Bell Rock." She didn't expect to have such a good time at a school function, but now she knew what to expect for the spring concert.

The audience applauded just as loud for the band as they had for the chorus. Cecilia stood up, and Lou, Trilby, and Lorelei all followed suit. When the applause died down, the chorus quickly scattered through the auditorium seeking their parents or friends. Cecilia tried to find Caroline, but it was difficult since everyone in the chorus was dressed the same. It was easy to find someone in a Santa hat, but it usually wasn't her. Trilby tapped on her shoulder and pointed to the front of the stage. Caroline was standing with her parents and the chorus director.

"Look," Lorelei was standing on her chair to see better, "There's Caroline!"

"Yes, and now the whole school knows," Lou looked up at Lorelei and offered her help off the chair. "Get down from there."

Cecilia knew they had to hurry because her mother had been very clear about how they needed to meet as soon as the concert ended. Trilby was the first to reach Caroline but waited for the chorus director to walk away. Lorelei ran right past her and grabbed Caroline like a wrestler taking down an opponent.

"You did so good!" Lorelei practically screamed into Caroline's ear.

"That was pretty impressive," Trilby managed to say as soon as Lorelei was finished.

"Wonderful, seriously. And so unexpected," Lou couldn't help but say.

"You were nervous, right?" Cecilia chimed in, "How did you do it? There were like a hundred people in here."

"More like fifty, but whatever," Lou noted.

Caroline waited for them to finish before she answered, "Thank you."

"No, really. How did you do that?" Cecilia was genuinely curious, "All eyes were on you. You were the show. How do you do it and not just freak out."

"Come on. It's not like it's a firing squad!" Caroline joked, but her friends just looked at each other nervously.

"Well, isn't it like a firing squad? You're alone in front of all those critical eyes just waiting to reject you," Lorelei was serious, but it was hard for Caroline to tell.

She looked at her friends' faces and realized they were genuinely concerned, "It's not like that. Your parents are out there. You think they're going to 'Boo' you or something." Again, her friends just looked at each other in silence. "There's too much to do to worry about all that. I have to stand up straight and breathe just right. I also have to keep the beat and remember all the words. I don't notice all the people when I concentrate on that stuff."

"But what if you mess up?" Trilby asked.

"Just keep going. There is another note and more to sing. You can't linger on just one note." Caroline was doing her best to comfort them.

Cecilia felt a pinch on the back of her elbow, "The concert is over, and you're not in the car." She recognized her mother's voice right away. "Beautiful job, dear," she praised Caroline and turned back to Cecilia, "This train is leaving the station, kid, move it."

All anyone could talk about in the car was Caroline. Cecilia nodded along with the conversation, but she kept thinking about how confident Caroline had been. Even when she was talking about it, she made the solo seem like it wasn't a big deal. By the time they got near Cecilia's house, everyone was overwhelmed by the experience and went home feeling satisfied.

about how confident Caroline had been. Even when she was talking about it, she made the solo seem like it wasn't a big deal. By the time they got near Cecilia's house, everyone was overwhelmed by the experience and went home feeling satisfied.

about how confident Caroline had been. Even when she was talking about it, she made the solo seem like it wasn't a big deal. By the time they got near Cecilia's house, everyone was overwhelmed by the experience and went home feeling satisfied.

Chapter Nine

After the night of the concert, everything changed for Cecilia. She practiced alone in her room every afternoon. If she started early enough, she didn't have to worry about her brother butting in. She still had a hard time warming up and practicing on her own. Before she lost her patience altogether, one day before class, she suggested to the rest of her friends that they get together after school and practice.

"That's a good idea," Lorelei was relieved to hear someone else needed extra practice.

"It worked out well when we were playing the recorders," Trilby reminded everyone.

"Seems like that was a lifetime ago," Cecilia observed.

"Yeah, I can't believe we even played those little toys," Lou agreed.

"It was a teaching tool," Lorelei corrected Lou.

"Come on. It was made of plastic. It was a toy," Lou repeated the word for effect. "But we worked hard to learn how to play those things, and we should work equally hard to learn how to play these horns." He waved his horn case around when he spoke.

None of them realized that Mr. Hamlin had overheard almost their entire conversation. He stepped closer to them and spoke casually over Cecilia's shoulder, "You know, the band room is open after school."

Cecilia turned around and tried not to look startled, "Oh, so we can practice here then."

"That's actually a good idea," Lou nodded at Mr. Hamlin.

Cecilia turned around so Mr. Hamlin couldn't see her face and snarled at Lou. She whispered, "Shut up," but then Lorelei put her two cents in.

"Can you help us if we need it?" she asked.

"I tutor other students and sometimes whole sections after school," Mr. Hamlin continued to speak over Cecilia's head. She quit snarling and looked back at him. "The band room is open to all band students as long as a teacher is present."

"This might work," Trilby had been thinking while Mr. Hamlin was talking. "We could get my mom to pick us up at least once a week."

Cecilia finally succumbed to the notion that this was going to happen and suggested, "I can talk Arion into it too." She couldn't believe she had said it out loud.

"Well, today you will get some new material to work on," Mr. Hamlin said as he herded his students closer to their chairs so he could begin class. "That's right. We've been working out of our practice books so far, but today I would like to pass out some sheet music." He reached toward the podium and grabbed a stack of papers. "I want us to play this for the spring concert." He made his way around the room and handed each section its part.

It was real music. Cecilia stared at the page in front of her. Line after line of musical notes and symbols. She would have to look up some of them again in her practice book.

"Make sure you keep up with your practice book and sheet music. Sometimes a folder helps keep things together," Mr. Hamlin suggested.

"How much sheet music will we get?" someone in the room asked.

Mr. Hamlin answered without identifying who asked, "I don't know. It depends. I want to try a couple of different songs before we decide what to play for the concert." He made his way to the back of the room to assign the percussion parts but continued to speak to the entire class. "We may play through this song a few times and decide we don't like it." He got back up to his podium and asked, "Where should we start?"

Answers came from all over the room.

"Set the tempo."

"Learn the notes."

Someone even asked, "What does this symbol mean?"

Amid the chaos, Cecilia noticed a lone hand in the air. She turned to see Thamyra Lirit sitting tall, ready to give the correct answer. "Warm-up."

"No matter what our objectives for the day may be, we will always warm-up," Mr. Hamlin explained.

Lorelei turned and gave Cecilia and Lou a quick grin under the music stand, which helped Cecilia relax a bit. During the warm-up, her confidence slowly began to build. Arion had complained at the dinner table about having to play the same thing over and over, but Cecilia found it quite comforting. She was drawn out of her shell whenever she played something familiar with the group. She crawled right back into that shell when it was time to close the practice books and focus on the sheet music. "Old Time March" was printed in bold at the top of the page. Cecilia didn't know where to start. What key was it in? Did she know all these notes?

"Let's jump right in," Mr. Hamlin said and stepped off the podium, "But we'll take it slow and easy. Take a look at the first two lines. No surprises. We've played in this key before, so you should be familiar with the notes. Take a minute to study the rhythm before we play." He made his way to the tuba section, where someone had a question.

Cecilia stared blankly at the sheet in front of her. Lou snapped her out of it when he picked up his pencil and made a few marks on the music.

"What are you doing?" she couldn't help but ask.

"Oh, well, see, this note is flat in this key unless it has a natural sign in front of it. I just put a little mark over the note, so I remember when we play." Lou explained and offered her his pencil so she could do the same thing.

"That is a great idea. I'll try that," Thamyra Lirit said as she began doing the same thing.

Cecilia noticed that everyone was working as a group to learn the new music. It was almost as if they had somehow done it all before. Mr. Hamlin got back on his podium, and the whole room went quiet without him having to instruct them to do so.

"For now, let's just put our horns in our laps, and we will clap the rhythm of the first two lines together," Mr. Hamlin put his hands together and made a clapping motion. "We're going to take it slow- 1, 2, 3, 4." He continued counting slowly, embedding the tempo in everyone's head. "This time, when I get to 4, be ready to follow the music and clap your part along with me. Remember, each section will play different parts, so try to concentrate on the notes on your page, not the ones you hear around you." He counted again, and everyone began clapping. To Cecilia, it sounded like a round of applause gone wrong, but Mr. Hamlin praised them when they had finished.

"Let's keep this same slow, steady tempo and play our horns. Drums, sit this one out for me." Then he said the four words he always says before they play, "Hands up, horns up."

Cecilia put her horn up, but she was nervous and shaky. She took a deep breath and tried to steady her grip on the horn. By the time Mr. Hamlin dropped his hands, she had her horn up, but she wasn't sure she was ready to play. She took a deep breath in, and when she exhaled, she played the same note as Lou and Thamyra. She didn't have long to be surprised or praise herself because she had to play the next note. The tempo seemed slower with the horns, so Cecilia had time to look at the note ahead of the one she was playing and get her fingers ready. She tried to focus on the music, notes, and rhythm, but she still managed to observe the sound of the entire class muddling through the new music. It was a disaster. Mr. Hamlin kept smiling and keeping the beat, so everyone kept playing. Before Cecilia could wish he would just cut them off and start over, they had reached the end of the second line. He lowered his hands, and the whole band sighed in relief.

"Don't sound so defeated. Your effort is what's important. You learn from your mistakes, so the more you make, the more you learn. We will all make the same mistakes together, and we will correct them together," Mr. Hamlin wasn't prepared to let the band give up on itself after having worked so hard. He had chosen one of his favorite songs to teach. Usually, the students enjoyed playing it also, but he had to push them to play while being patient with their efforts. "Just the drums now. You guys ready back there?" He counted off the same tempo and led them through the same two lines of the song. He cut them off but never lowered his hands, "Everyone and drums, let's do this together one time."

This time it sounded even worse to Cecilia. She tried to focus on the notes she was playing, but the drums were pounding, and squawks and squeaks were coming from every corner of the room. When he cut them off, they sat in shocked silence. After playing a warm-up song they all knew and played well, it was difficult to listen to the sound they were making now.

"Okay. Let's hear the woodwinds clap the rhythm for me. Brass and drums, take a look at your music and follow along silently." Mr. Hamlin used his most encouraging tone.

Cecilia looked over at Lou, but he was leaning close to the music stand studying his part. Thamyra was looking at her music and fingering chart to practice the notes. When Mr. Hamlin counted off the beat, Cecilia looked back at her music. She quickly noticed that the flutes, clarinets, and saxophones played something very different from what she had in front of her. No wonder it sounded so jumbled. Now she knew what their part sounded like. She knew what rhythm to ignore when she was trying to find the beat.

"What do you think, trumpets? Could you join us? You have a very important part here at the beginning." Mr. Hamlin came to the trumpet section and clapped along with their part. It helped Cecilia to hear what it was supposed to sound like. She noticed that she could hear the song even though they were clapping. The rhythm was starting to solidify and become the music that was on the page.

Mr. Hamlin isolated the bass section and clapped out their part with them and then let the drums play through it on their instruments. He was trying not to get too ahead of himself. The band had been doing very well, and he was excited for them. Nobody had put their horn down in defeat or glared at him in confusion. Everyone was still trying.

"One more time together. Hands up, horns up," he instructed with a grin. He knew it would be better this time, and they would be surprised at what they were capable of.

Cecilia couldn't believe how serious everyone was being. Even Lorelei seemed on task, and she usually passed notes halfway through class. Cecilia looked at Mr. Hamlin to get the beat and then focused on the music.

This time it all sounded very different. Not only were most of the notes and rhythms correct, but everyone seemed more confident somehow. They had repeated it so much that now they didn't have to focus on so many little things at once. The tubas and trombones were bolder with their booming bass notes, and the saxophone section really stood out. Cecilia could feel it all coming together as they played better than she had ever heard them play. It was still a bit of a train wreck, but it was a beautiful and well-orchestrated wreck.

Mr. Hamlin cut the band off and began clapping for them. His own little round of applause for the group. "That's what it's supposed to sound like," he commended the class' efforts. "Don't lose this music. We'll keep working on it. I know the bell hasn't rung yet, but I've gotten word that you guys aren't making it to class on time. It's my fault. From now on, we'll try to finish a minute or two early, so you have a chance to pack up before the bell rings. Get your things together, and nobody leave until that bell rings."

"Wasn't that awesome!" Cecilia said to Lou as soon as Mr. Hamlin was done.

"It was awful," Thamyra Lirit interrupted.

"It was fun, though," Cecilia wasn't going to let Thamyra discredit the glory of the moment.

"Better than I expected," Lou finally answered.

"Oh, yeah, I can't believe we pulled that off," Lorelei had overheard and helped herself to the conversation. "It was real music with all those parts and the drums and everything."

Cecilia quickly stuffed her horn in its case and got her backpack in order. This time she would be waiting for Caroline after class. She followed Lou and Lorelei to the front of the room where Trilby was already waiting.

"You guys sure sound great. Too bad nobody can hear the flute section," Trilby whined to her friends as soon as they were in earshot.

"Hey, every part is important," Lorelei said with a smile.

"Of course, you say that. Everyone can hear you saxes. We are a whisper among wails," Trilby continued to pout. "I guess that's why we get front row."

"Come on now," Lou sounded encouraging, "You are a part of it and no more important than any other part."

Trilby tried to get into the same spirit as the rest of her friends, "Maybe you're right."

The bell rang, and they were off like soda shooting out of a shaken bottle. Cecilia felt like she was thrown into the hallway, but she had beaten Caroline.

"Whoa, early bird today. How'd that happen?" Caroline beamed as she led the way out of the music hall.

"Apparently, I'm not the only one who gets to class late. He let us get ready before the bell," she explained, and Caroline came to a dead stop.

"What?" Cecilia looked at her, "We are going to be early for the first time all year, and you're stopping."

Her nostrils flared, and Cecilia knew she must have been eyeballing the Ditham brothers. She looked over and saw Ben and Moe poised and ready to pick on them as they tried to pass. Caroline snapped out of her trance and slowly began walking toward Ben and Moe.

"What are you doing?" Cecilia asked, following behind her, "If we pass on the far right, we might get by them."

"Just stay behind them while I talk, okay," Caroline suggested.

"I guess," she managed to say as they approached the two boys.

Caroline took her position in front of Ben and Moe and immediately began insulting them so they would both look at her. Cecilia still didn't know what her role in all this was. What was she supposed to do? She watched Caroline carefully, hoping that she would give her some kind of signal. What was the signal? She watched Caroline poke Ben on the shoulder, and he took a step back away from her. She did it again to Moe, and he also reacted by taking a step back. Cecilia grinned the moment she realized all she had to do was put her trumpet case down, step back, and watch the show.

Casually she left the case sitting on the floor half a step behind the Ditham boys. They took no notice of her because Caroline was doing a good job keeping their attention. She had also gotten the attention of a few passing students who joined Cecilia like a little mini audience. Caroline poked one more time, but this time she poked both Ben and Moe at the same time. She thrust both her arms straight out in front of her and poked with just enough force not to shove. Just like before, both boys stepped back, but their feet met Cecilia's horn case this time. Both were so surprised and confused that they fell. They fell into each other, and then they fell back onto the hard linoleum floor. The bystanders clapped for Caroline and her splendid show. Cecilia picked her horn case up as casually as she had placed it. She joined Caroline, and both shared a high five before continuing on to class.

"Now, *that's* a reason to get to class early!" Cecilia couldn't help but say as they glanced back at the mayhem they had created together.

"I've never seen anything more perfect than those two idiots lying on the floor like that!" Caroline stated triumphantly.

"I knew carrying this thing around would pay off," Cecilia held up her horn case and giggled.

"Is it heavy?" Caroline asked as she took it from Cecilia's grip. "Oh, it *is* heavy. How do you hold it up all during class?"

"We don't hold them up the entire time." Cecilia explained sarcastically, "And we get to take them out of the case."

Caroline handed her horn back to her, "Well, it sure served us well today."

"I hope it serves me well for the spring concert," Cecilia replied.

"Don't worry about all that. It's like months away," Caroline said as they walked into class.

"I know. We are learning real sheet music now," she put her horn case in the back of the room and took her seat.

"Us, too." Caroline wanted her to know they were all on the same page. "We'll all be there doing the same thing. It'll be fine. You'll see."

Just before the bell rang, Mrs. Shannon appeared in the doorway, "Well, it's good to see everyone in class on time today." Cecilia and Caroline just smiled at each other and turned their attention to the front of the room.

***

It only took a week for Cecilia to convince Arion to pick her and her friends up after practice. She had to agree to do his stinky laundry for the rest of the month, but it was worth the sacrifice to her. She was relieved to see that her friends were just as serious about the concert as she was. Even Lorelei was concentrating on practice instead of running her mouth. Lou kept them in line and made sure they stayed on task.

On their first afternoon practice, they worked on "Old Time March" and were way ahead of the game the next day in class. Sometimes another student would join them. Trilby was always eager to introduce another instrument to the group. One time half the flute section showed up to work on a solo part they might get to try out for. Another time a saxophone player stayed after with them and helped Lorelei with her part on their new song "Nocturne." But the day that the tuba player showed up, everything changed.

"Hey Leo," Lou called across the almost empty band room, "You can play with us if you want. We were going to go through the sheet music from class."

Leo silently wandered over and sat in an empty chair next to Lou, "Thanks, not much time to practice at home."

He mumbled softly, but Lorelei replied quite loudly, "That's cool. We used to do this when we were playing the recorders."

"You know, I think this is the first time we've ever played with some bass," Cecilia noted. "This should be interesting."

And it was. It was the same, but there was more to it. Leo's bass notes complemented the rest of the group, and soon they were exploring different ways to manipulate the music. They would play through once really slow and then play it fast the next time. It didn't take long for Mr. Hamlin to catch an earful of what was going on, and he stepped out of his office to take a look. He watched quietly as his students experimented with their abilities. He tried not to interrupt, but Lorelei noticed him right away.

"What do you think?" she asked him.

"I definitely hear improvements throughout the group," he commended. "You know what, though, there are just enough of you to make up a small ensemble. I've even got a piece of music you could try together. Let's look here in the library."

He motioned for them to follow and stepped to a small door just to the left of the cubbyholes. Cecilia hadn't noticed the door before, but certainly, it had always been there. There was nothing special about it. A tiny sliver of a window was covered, so there was no way to see inside. Taped to the top of the door was a small piece of paper with the word "Library" written on it. Mr. Hamlin used a key to open it, so Cecilia assumed that it stayed locked.

Even though he had called it a library, there were no books in the room. Leo, Lou, and Trilby didn't try to squeeze into the little room, but Cecilia and Lorelei helped themselves. File drawers lined the tiny closet of a space. Stray music lay on top of and stuck to the sides of the drawers. There weren't any labels, but somehow Mr. Hamlin knew exactly which drawer to go to.

"This is it." He held up a sheet of the song, "It was written for a small ensemble. The five of you should be just enough. Take it out there and have a look."

Cecilia couldn't believe it. Not only was she enjoying practice, but Mr. Hamlin was handing out special music just for them. She loved how he called them an ensemble. She sat with Lou and began looking over the music. She immediately noticed that there were two different trumpet parts. She was familiar with playing different parts within the section to create harmony, but that was with the whole band. Who would play which part?

"What do you think?" Lou asked with a seemingly indifferent tone, "Rock, paper, scissors." He held up his fist and gestured accordingly.

"You can play the first part," Cecilia immediately surrendered.

"Let's shoot for it," he insisted.

"The harmony will be stronger with you on top," she explained.

She suddenly noticed that Mr. Hamlin wasn't directing them. She was used to his presence in front of her and his voice instructing her. He was still there but standing silently in the doorway of his office. He remained there until Trilby motioned him over.

"What does that mean?" She asked, pointing to her music.

"It's when you flutter between two notes," he put his hands in the air and played an invisible flute. "It's supposed to sound like birds tweeting." Trilby tried it immediately.

"It does sound like birds," Lorelei looked up from her music stand for the first time since they got the new music.

"The song is called 'Springtime Jubilee,'" Mr. Hamlin pointed to the title of the song. "The instruments make the sounds of a spring day. Give it a try. The tempo is supposed to be pretty upbeat but take it slow." Then he stepped back. He didn't put his hands in the air and count. He watched. He let them do the work themselves.

Lou was unfazed by Mr. Hamlin's absence and reviewed his music again. "Slow and easy it is, then. Is everyone ready? Leo?"

Leo looked up from behind his enormous instrument, "I'm used to the clapping like we do in class."

"Good idea!" Lorelei agreed. She put her horn in her lap and her hands together.

Lou counted off a steady tempo, and the clapping began. No one was listening to the other. Each one of them was intent on their part. It was hard to hear how the song was supposed to go because it was so jumbled. Cecilia didn't even know if she was clapping the correct rhythm. She wasn't the only one because none of them stopped clapping at the same time.

"Uh, let's try that again. Even slower this time," Lou clapped the beat and cued everyone when to join him.

The slower tempo made it easy to decipher the pattern of notes. Leo was much more confident the second time and pounded the bass on his music stand. Trilby was having a hard time clapping like chirping birds, but she was doing her best.

They almost finished together the second time. Leo's loud beat helped keep them all on track. Lou used his pencil to make a few notes on his music and looked up at the group.

"Let's play it," Trilby insisted. "My mom will be here to pick us up any minute."

Cecilia looked at the clock and was shocked at how quickly time had passed. It wasn't the first time it had happened while she was practicing, even if she was just by herself. She was so focused on what she was doing that she lost track of time. She wondered if that meant she really liked it.

"Same tempo, okay," Leo suggested.

All five of them raised their horns. Lou tapped out the tempo with his foot and used the bell of his horn to start the others. First came Trilby's chirping bird, which sounded realistic to Cecilia. Leo's tuba kept a pace that was like the heartbeat of the world that each of them could feel all the way to the toes. The trumpets shined through like the sun and were just as cheerful.

Underneath it all was Lorelei's sax buzzing around like happy bugs on a spring day.

Mr. Hamlin was right. The song painted a picture, and they could all see it.

"A little work, and that will be perfect for the spring concert," he suggested as soon as they had finished.

They all looked at each other in disbelief. Cecilia kept looking from the music to each of the faces in the group. She couldn't decide if this was a good thing. Everyone mulled over the idea while they packed up their instruments.

"It's not like it's a solo," Lorelei said with some apprehension.

"It does sound pretty neat," Trilby added.

"I can only meet one day a week," Leo explained.

Lou addressed the group, "So one day we practice songs for class, and the other we work on the ensemble piece."

Cecilia looked at Lou, "We're going to do this for the concert? We're going to play 'Springtime Jubilee.'" She had to say the words. She still couldn't picture herself sitting in front of an audience with just her music stand to shield her.

"I'll keep an ear on you while you practice," Mr. Hamlin stepped toward the group, "But it sounds like a plan to me."

***

It was all anyone could talk about in the car. Mrs. Euterpek could hardly hear to over-hear what they were all going on about. As they got closer to the Banbury house, she started to figure it out.

"What song?" She managed to bellow over all the conversation.

"Oh, Spring, something," Lorelei rattled off.

"'Springtime Jubilee,'" Trilby corrected.

"It will be us and a tuba player, Leo," Lou explained.

They pulled up in front of Cecilia's house, and both she and Lou got out. Mrs. Euterpek popped the trunk, and they got their horns. Cecilia stepped near the window.

"Thanks for the ride," she said politely.

"You're welcome, dear," Mrs. Euterpek replied. "Tell your mom 'Hi' for me."

Lou waved from the curb, and Cecilia joined him as the car pulled away.

"You don't want to do the ensemble thing, do you?" he could always read her like a book.

"Here's the thing," she took a breath before explaining, "I don't want to say no. Either you guys won't get to play at all, or I'll get replaced so you can play."

He knew she was right, "Are you going to play?" She sounded so unsure he couldn't help but ask.

"I just said I have to," she put her horn and book bag down on the porch.

"You don't *have* to do anything," he continued to prod her for an answer. "Do you want to play?"

"I guess I will if it's you guys," she said in defeat.

"Do you know how many times we will play that song from now until the concert?" He didn't wait for her to answer. "Probably enough to memorize it. It will be like second nature by the time we get it down."

"I'm in," she threw her arms in the air and made a gesture to stop the band from playing, but it didn't stop him from talking.

"Really? Because we don't want to sound…" he paused to search for the right adjective.

She interrupted him before he got the chance, "Why do you think I'm so scared to play? I don't want to be embarrassed. We will do it together. All of us. I'm in."

He looked her in the eye to confirm she was serious and nodded in approval. She watched the back of him as he walked toward his house. She knew he would go right home and work on the new song. That's how Lou was. She looked down at her own horn and pointed at it as if she were scolding it for something. She dragged it in with her books and shut the door behind her.

"How was practice?" Arion asked in a sing-song voice when he heard his sister come in.

"Interesting, I guess," she mumbled, but her brother heard her anyway.

"Oh, what was so interesting," he inquired sarcastically.

Cecilia ventured to tell him the truth just to get his reaction, "Mr. Hamlin gave us an ensemble piece and we're going to play it at the spring concert."

"What ensemble?" he asked in his regular voice.

"You know, Lou and Trilby and Lorelei and Leo, the tuba player," she recited the list and counted along with her fingers.

"You and your friends get to play a song at your end-of-year concert," Arion was trying to get all the facts straight.

"We're going to play "Springtime Jubilee" for the Spring Concert," she filled in the blanks her brother wasn't filling in for himself.

"What? Did Mr. Hamlin say this?" he asked.

"Yeah," she shrugged, "He heard us practicing and said we could play this song."

"That's a pretty big compliment," he tried to impress upon her how important it was. "You must be good." He tousled her hair around and went up to his room.

Cecilia shrugged again, but she hadn't thought about it the way her brother had. Mr. Hamlin didn't ask anyone else. He asked them.

Chapter Ten

Cecilia was suddenly very busy. Between the new music and her new friends, she barely had time for schoolwork. Sometimes she thought that school just got in the way of all the other stuff she was trying to do. But she continued to exert maximum effort to guarantee everything got done. The school year was winding down, so she had to make time to practice for the concert, study for a few big tests, and write a book report.

Practice was the most important thing on her list. She always made sure she made it to after-school practice and made time to practice at home. She was drawn to all kinds of music. Tapping her foot to keep the beat was now second nature. Whether she was listening or playing, her foot was tapping. She had also gotten into the habit of clutching her horn to her chest when they were taking a break from practice.

Cecilia's emotions became more conflicted as the day of the concert approached. When she felt something, she felt the exact opposite but at the same time. She was scared, terrified even, but she was also happy. She was nervous but somehow confident. She knew she wasn't perfect and that she had her weaknesses, but at the same time, she felt very strong.

She practiced the ensemble piece diligently every afternoon. She wanted to make sure she and the rest of the group sounded the best they could. She didn't want to be the one that would mess it up for the rest of them.

Leo, in particular, seemed more excited than the rest of the group. His catchphrase became "One more time." Trilby was the same way, but only because she wanted to be perfect. Cecilia couldn't tell if Trilby was having fun. She was so focused on the music that she wasn't getting a chance to enjoy the experience. Lorelei had turned over a new leaf as far as her practice manners went. She kept her conversations until after practice and didn't interrupt others when things got dull for a minute. Lou was the hub of it all. He memorized his part right away, so he helped everyone work out their part at one point or another. Cecilia knew he had walked Lorelei through the entire song when they first started practicing. They would jokingly call him "Maestro" when he directed them during ensemble practice.

The weekend of the concert was as busy as any that school year. That Friday, she had to present her science project to the class. She built a model of an atom out of foam and paint. It turned out pretty good, and the presentation got her an A. But she couldn't let her guard down just yet because the Spring Concert was the following afternoon. She even had to spend her Sunday finishing her book report for Monday. She didn't remember sixth grade being this complicated.

She had the hardest time getting to sleep that night. Besides being overly excited about the concert, the ensemble song "Spring Jubilee" kept playing over and over in her head. It made it almost impossible to get to sleep. Once she finally did doze off, she dreamt of the concert the next day. She was playing along with the whole band when slowly, people began to get up and leave. Before long, the gym was completely empty.

Cecilia woke up in a cold sweat. She tiptoed to the bathroom for a quick drink of water. She stared at herself in the mirror and replayed the dream to herself in her head. She was relieved that the dream meant she wanted to play with the ensemble. She feared that something would prevent them from playing.

She woke up early the next morning. She couldn't help it. She lay in bed and stared at her trumpet case for almost a half hour before she got up. She kept looking at it as she got dressed. The band had to wear black and white, so she had a black skirt and a white shirt ready to wear.

It was still early when she opened her door to go downstairs. She hated how time went by so fast during practice, and so slow any other time. Breakfast was ready, but everyone else was still in their pajamas.

"Jumping the gun a little, aren't we?" her dad asked when she walked into the kitchen.

"This is what I had hung up to wear today, so it's what I'm wearing," she explained flatly.

"Cover that shirt with a napkin, so you don't get syrup on it," her mother suggested as she served Cecilia fresh warm waffles and bacon.

Cecilia hadn't thought about spilling something on her outfit until now, "Shoot."

"I tell you what, I am ready to see my kid sister play in the band," Arion said as he finished making a tiny waffle and bacon sandwich covered in maple syrup.

"You're coming?" Cecilia asked after a big gulp of milk.

"We're all coming, dear. Your first concert is important. We all want to be there," her dad said each sentence between sips of coffee.

Cecilia stared at her waffle and thought about all the other parents, brothers, sisters, grandparents, aunts, uncles, and family friends attending. After all, that's why it was held in the gym. She poked at the rest of her breakfast and tossed the rest out after everyone else had left the kitchen. She sat in front of the TV until her mother called, and it was time to go.

The car ride was quiet. Cecilia's parents talked back and forth, and Arion sat silently in the back seat next to her. She couldn't believe he hadn't driven his own car, but her mother may have insisted he ride with the family. When they pulled up to the school, it looked as busy as a regular school day. Parents were milling around the parking lot, bragging about their child's musical talents. The students were making their way to Music Hall to warm up before the concert.

Cecilia's parents both hugged her, "Good luck, hon."

"You've got your own little cheering section right here," her brother said reassuringly.

"Thanks, you guys," Cecilia was grateful for their efforts. "See you after the thing." Once again, she got that firing squad feeling. She had just said goodbye to her loved ones, and now she was following the rest of the prisoners to what will be the end of their lives. The daydream faded as she got closer to the music hall. There were students everywhere. Some were in band, and some were in chorus. She could tell the difference because the chorus wore khaki, and the band wore black.

First, she noticed Leo, who seemed to be trying to hide behind his huge tuba. Cecilia almost wished that her horn was big enough to use as a shield.

"Over here," Caroline yelled in her direction and waved her hand wildly in the air.

She walked closer and saw Caroline standing with Lou and Trilby, "Hello, everybody."

"Are you ready?" Trilby asked excitedly.

"I can see you are. Where do we go?" Cecilia looked at all the faces of the assembled mob around her.

"Don't know. We've been standing around waiting for instructions," Lou replied.

"Why don't we just go in the band room?" Cecilia couldn't help but ask.

"Remember that first day when there were no chairs? De ja vu," Trilby pointed toward the open band room door. Sure enough, it was completely empty. No chairs, no music stands, and no drums. It was a sad sight to see such a large room suddenly so empty.

"I guess they already took everything to the gym," Cecilia stated.

"Yeah, so where are two band classes going to sit to warm-up?" Trilby countered.

"Oh, I didn't think about that," Cecilia looked to Lou for a bit of wisdom or at least a distraction from the stress of the situation.

He seemed indifferent about the issue but had no problem shifting the focus of the conversation, "Look." He pointed over Caroline's shoulder. "Lorelei is finally here."

"You're late," Trilby scolded the minute she was within earshot.

"Am not," Lorelei protested. "You're just mad because I wasn't here when you were."

Trilby shot her a sharp gaze before asking, "Did you bring everything?"

"What everything? I've got my horn," she picked her horn up and waved it around to prove its existence.

"What about your music?" Trilby prodded.

"What are you, her mother?" Caroline asked.

"We're playing the ensemble piece, and I want to make sure she has the music, okay," she quickly shifted her attention back to Lorelei.

"Who do you think I am? What kind of band student would I be without sheet music? It's right here." Lorelei flipped open her saxophone case right there on the music hall floor. All that lay in the case was her shiny instrument.

"Where? Lorelei, where is the music?" Trilby started to sound genuinely concerned.

She looked up from the horn case, purely astonished by what wasn't lying in front of her. "It was here. I practiced yesterday afternoon, and I put everything back in my case." Her gaze shifted to each of her friends in search of support.

"You better hope Mr. Hamlin has another copy of that part. I invited my entire family to this," Trilby's voice began to crescendo as her anger became apparent to all the observers.

Lorelei sat on the floor and watched as Trilby squawked around like an angry chicken. She put her hands on her hips and paced up and down in front of Lorelei's open saxophone case. She waved her hands in the air every now and then. Lorelei had managed to get her pretty worked up about the whole thing. Caroline and Cecilia looked at her pleadingly, hoping she could somehow calm Trilby. Lorelei shuffled her reeds and mouthpiece around while Trilby berated her for her unforgivable error.

"I mean, seriously, what have we been working so hard for, huh?" Trilby found a moment to take a break.

"Are you done?" Lorelei looked up from her spot on the floor.

"Not really, but what do you want?" Trilby seemed out of breath from her rant.

Lorelei didn't say anything. She motioned for Trilby to come around to her. Lorelei lifted the horn out of its case and handed it to her. She reluctantly took it but continued to look down at Lorelei disapprovingly.

"Does your horn case do this?" She asked as she reached in and revealed a small compartment. She waved her arm with a dramatic flourish as she held all of her music and her practice book in her hand.

"What? Do you think that's funny?" Trilby seemed more angry than relieved.

"Yeah, actually." Lorelei laughed as she spoke. "Break the tension, you know." Soon they were all sharing a giggle, and Trilby couldn't help but join in.

Cecilia was starting to let her guard down and have a good time until she saw Mr. Hamlin come out of the band room.

"It's time," she said to her friends as if it were a goodbye.

"I better get with the rest of the chorus. Good luck, everybody," Caroline said encouragingly before walking away.

Lou and Trilby stood closer to Lorelei and Cecilia and silently waited for further instruction. They didn't wait long.

"Okay. I need everyone to pay attention," Mr. Hamlin stood next to the chorus teacher, who nodded in agreement with whatever he said. "Chorus will warm-up across the hall in the science lab. Beginner and advanced bands will warm-up together in the chorus room."

The students parted like ripples through water. Anyone wearing khaki went left, and anyone wearing black went right. It was a beautifully unrehearsed ballet. Once in the chorus room, Cecilia immediately noticed that there were chairs, just not enough for the hundred-odd students.

"Some of you will have to stand and even share music. This is not permanent. We just need to warm-up before we get to the gym. Let's do the B flat scale and arpeggio." Mr. Hamlin instructed and waited for everyone to get sorted into their proper section.

When it was all said and done, Cecilia was squished between two eighth graders that she didn't even know. She put her horn to her mouth, but she was shaking so badly she was afraid of breaking a tooth on her mouthpiece. She put her horn down and took a deep breath. So much was happening so fast. One minute she was laughing with her friends, and now she was crammed between two total strangers. She wanted to turn her horn upside down and throw up in it. Before she could work up the chunks, Mr. Hamlin's hands were in the air.

It wasn't as familiar as the warm-up they did in class. She didn't like sharing music with someone she didn't know. She felt intimidated by the advanced students. It was over as quickly as it started, and again, she listened intently to Mr. Hamlin's instructions.

"Here's how today will go," He tried to sound calm, but he always got excited before a concert. "Advanced band will play first. Beginner band, you will sit in the reserved section on the left side of the bleachers. Then the chorus will perform. After that, the beginner band will switch places with the 8th graders. That's it. Stay with your section, and we will walk together to the gym." He stepped down and showed the flutes to the door.

Cecilia waited so she could walk with Lou. It didn't comfort her at all, though. The butterflies in her stomach were tossing and tumbling around inside her. There was a light buzz of conversation, but for the most part, the march down exploratory hall was quiet. Those who weren't nervous were excited, and vice versa.

When they entered the gym, Cecilia was utterly shocked at the number of people that were in the audience. All the parents and teachers and relatives were waiting for the big show. She couldn't believe that many people were interested in the band and chorus, but that was only because, deep down, she was hoping the audience would be smaller. She joined the rest of the 7th grade band in the bleachers and watched and waited with the rest of the audience.

The band started right up. Cecilia had always been amazed at how big they sounded. Everything was so over the top. She couldn't remember the 7th grade band having that big sound. She looked down and noticed Lou tapping his foot along with the beat. She smiled to herself and focused on the band again. She told herself it would take a while for both the advanced band and the chorus to perform, but she was quite wrong.

The band began its final song, and the chorus filed onto the risers set up for them. When the song was finished, the chorus began right away. Once again, everything was happening very fast when she wanted time would pass more slowly. The chorus performed beautifully and quickly. Then it was time to face the music.

The advanced band filed out as the beginner band filed in. Everyone appeared to know where they were supposed to be. Once again, Cecilia thought the moment seemed somehow rehearsed.

She couldn't believe how serious and still everyone was sitting, seemingly ready for what was about to happen. Lou put a copy of the song "Nocturne" on their shared music stand. She scanned the music before raising her horn to her lips. This time she didn't shake as much, but she was fighting to keep her arms from quivering.

She looked up at Mr. Hamlin and was immediately relieved by the look on his face. He was not tense. He did not look nervous. In fact, the more Cecilia inspected his expression she began to realize that he was, in fact, happy. Not once had it occurred to her that this was a happy day and a good thing. She had been dreading embarrassment and rejection. There was no room for acceptance or joy. He gave the whole band a once over as if he were trying to spread his happiness to the rest of them. Some of them caught it, including Cecilia.

She took a deep breath and played one note at a time. She followed her music and periodically looked up at Mr. Hamlin to check the beat. It turns out that she thought she was afraid of the concert when in fact, it was all she wanted. The whole group was breathing and playing together. She could feel the magic in the air. Sometimes she thought she saw it coming from Mr. Hamlin's hands as he stroked the air with his baton.

When he brought his hands back down, Cecilia heard the most beautiful sound. It was applause. She looked into the audience and saw the firing squad she feared so much clapping and praising their performance.

Lou looked at her and grabbed his music before heading to the five chairs set up specifically for the ensemble. Mr. Hamlin gave them a brief introduction as they took their seats.

"This small ensemble is made up of some pretty devoted students. I heard them practicing one afternoon and couldn't resist giving them the opportunity to play one of my favorite songs of the season. Ladies and Gentlemen, the 7th grade beginner band ensemble playing 'Springtime Jubilee.'"

Cecilia looked at the faces in the semi-circle. They all looked terrified. It made her feel better to know they were sick with nerves too. She waited for Lou to tap out the tempo, but he counted it off this time.

"One, two, three, four," he managed to say before putting his horn to his lips.

Trilby's birds flittered all over the gym and performed amazing acrobatics in the basketball hoops that hung from the high ceiling. Then Leo's tuba opened the room, and suddenly they were sitting in a blooming daisy meadow. When Lorelei began, the bugs came out from their hiding places in the grass and flowers. All this was exposed in the bright brassy sunlight made by Lou and Cecilia's trumpets. It was all there. The picture in Cecilia's head was now in the air for the whole world to see.

She was a little sad when the song was over, but that quickly turned to utter exhilaration when she heard the audience applaud for her and her friends. They looked at each other with beaming expressions of accomplishment.

Cecilia was amazed with the entire experience and her ability to conform to it. She had played in a small ensemble in front of a hundred parents. As soon as they were seated, it was time to play the final song, "Old Time March." Her trumpet played itself. She didn't even feel like she was holding it up. It was just floating in front of her, doing all the work.

Mr. Hamlin cut the band off with his hands and brought them down by his side. The audience burst into applause. This time Cecilia looked at the crowd and noticed it was her friends and their parents and some teachers and people she didn't even know. They were all clapping for them. Caroline was standing with the chorus giving a miniature standing ovation. Her parents waved proudly, and she noticed Arion was even clapping.

Cecilia loved this feeling. She wanted to feel this way as much as possible. For once in her short life, she knew what she wanted to do. She wanted to practice and play. She was officially a band geek.

The End

time Cecilia looked at the crowd she noticed her friends and their parents and some teachers and people she didn't even know. They were all clapping for them. Carolyn was standing with the Chorus giving a [illegible] standing ovation. Her [illegible] [illegible] proudly and she noticed Maria was even clapping.

Cecilia loved this feeling. She wanted to feel this way as much as possible. [illegible] in her short life, she knew what she wanted to do. She wanted to [illegible] and [illegible] she was [illegible] [illegible] hard work.

The End

Acknowledgments

The book you hold in your hands would not have been possible without the friendship, advice, and support of my favorite local bookseller Tracie Harris at The Book House in Mableton, GA. She endured endless questions and text sessions, not to mention the occasional pep talks, without which I wouldn't have had the courage to publish this story. Special thanks to Russell Holbrook for his advice and expertise as well.

My favorite memories from my school days are focused on the band directors who made a memorable impression on me: Mr. Gary Dawson and Mr. Tom MacArthur.

My husband, Chuck Hayes, never doubted me for a second, no matter what crazy idea I had. His love and encouragement kept me going even when I wasn't sure where those paths would lead. Although I no longer play, my husband has kept music in my life, and for that, I am eternally grateful.

Lastly, I must thank my parents, Kitty Price and Roland Yarbrough, for always giving me the opportunity to explore, learn and grow as much as they did so I could become who I am.

About the Author

Lara Hope Hayes is a proud former band geek. She traded her sheet music for a love of reading and writing. She graduated from Kennesaw State University with a degree in English. She still loves music, and although she does not play anymore, her husband is a professional drummer and has kept music in her life. She lives in Atlanta, GA, with her husband, dogs, cats, and chickens.

Follow Lara Hope Hayes on Social Media

Instagram @larahopehayes

Twitter @larahopehayes

Facebook: Youth Fiction Fantasy Writer

CPSIA information can be obtained
at www.ICGtesting.com
Printed in the USA
LVHW032026261222
735863LV00003B/392

9 798218 091286